SECRET SANTA

LAURA GLYNN

Laura

I hope you enjoy the book!

First published 2022
by Rowanvale Books Ltd
The Gate
Keppoch Street
Roath
Cardiff
CF24 3JW
www.rowanvalebooks.com

A CIP catalogue record for this book is available from the British Library.

Paperback ISBN: 978-1-913662-70-7
eBook ISBN: 978-1-913662-71-4

To Ian, Mum, Dad, Gemma, Carla, Sam and Nan.
Thank you for supporting and believing in me.

With love xx

CHAPTER ONE

The log fell in the grate with a crackle as Lizzy Chesterfield busied herself with her morning routine. She had fifteen minutes before she was officially late for her shift at the Wooden Spoon Coffee Shop.

With a slice of toast hanging from her mouth and only one arm in a coat sleeve, she ran out of her country cottage, hastily slammed the front door shut and clambered into her car, sending a silent prayer of thanks to the heavens that she didn't need to scrape any ice off the windscreen. After two miles down winding country lanes, between vast expanses of frosty fields, she came to the little village of Dovebury, which had been her home since childhood. She pulled to a screeching halt in one of the parking spaces outside the coffee shop, jumped out the car and dashed through the door with a minute to spare, much to the despair of her boss and best friend since school, Claire.

"Lizzy, you seriously need to get more organised. The way you rush around, you'll have an accident one day!"

"Oh, stop worrying. I'm a lot better than I used to be! I'm no longer late anymore!" Lizzy winked as she tapped the watch on her wrist. She made her way through the tables and chairs into the kitchen area, where she hung up her coat and put on her apron.

Rolling her eyes, Claire began arranging the freshly baked cakes and pastries behind the glass display case under the counter.

"Don't forget we need to stay late tonight and bake the cookies for the school's nativity play refreshment stand." Claire looked pointedly at Lizzy, who had a slightly bewildered look on her face. "You did promise you'd help!"

"I haven't forgotten — I'll need to run a few errands at lunch time," Lizzy swiftly acknowledged as she tied her brunette curls into a messy bun and straightened out her clothes. "Hmmm, I might also call Peter and see if he can give us a hand."

"Oh, good idea. He's a dab hand with a piping bag — remember those gingerbread houses he and his brother Mark used to make for the annual gingerbread contest? They always won!" Claire exclaimed with a pained look on her face. "This year, I am determined to beat those Henley brothers! I will be the winner at least once!"

Shaking her head, Lizzy began arranging the table-cloths and decorations as Claire opened the door and welcomed the first customers of the day. The Wooden Spoon Coffee Shop was a quaint little tearoom set back from the main village square. It had been a tearoom for as long as anyone residing in the village could remember and had been in Claire's family for generations, each owner passing the legacy down to their child to carry on the tradition.

When Claire's mother and father had retired to a community on a Spanish golf course by the sea, Claire had been apprehensive about taking over the family business, but Lizzy had offered her a helping hand. For the five years since, she had worked alongside Claire baking desserts, making sandwiches and serving the customers. Between them, they had redecorated the aging tearoom, bringing in new furniture and brightening up the walls with a fresh coat of paint and trinkets depicting the history of the place, including old tea sets, jugs and plates hung on the wall. With the stone, inglenook fireplace and a large grandfather clock in the corner, Lizzy and Claire had managed to create a warm and cosy atmosphere that was the centre of the village social scene throughout the year.

The morning rush was almost over when Bob, the postman, came through the door, whistling a Christmas tune. He was a tall, slim man in his fifties, with greying hair, a shaggy beard and a weather-beaten face. Lizzy had always had a soft spot for Bob. She could remember as a child peering through the net curtains on the morning of her birthday, waiting for the moment she would see Bob strolling down the garden path with a bag full of cards and parcels for her from family all over the country. She would run to the front door and pull it open with such excitement that Bob often joked, even to this day, that she could have pulled it off its hinges. Bob would smile and hand Lizzy the pile of cards and packages, all addressed to her, and watch as she ran back indoors to show her parents what she had received.

"Good morning, ladies, how are we today? Can I have a latte and a Danish pastry to go, please?" Bob perched on a counter stool while he sorted through his postbag, separating the letters and packages for Claire and Lizzy.

"I have a surprise for you today, Lizzy!" he exclaimed with raised eyebrows. "Do you seriously still write letters to Santa?"

He handed Lizzy a handwritten envelope with a "From the North Pole" stamp in the top right-hand corner.

A little perplexed, Lizzy opened the red wax seal on the back. "Of course I don't. It must be a mistake with the address. It's probably for a local child who wrote to Santa asking for a Christmas wish and gave the wrong address for the reply."

The letter was written on thick parchment. The penmanship was beautiful—copperplate and almost magical. Lizzy began to read the letter aloud.

My dearest Lizzy,

For many years, I have dreamed of telling you how I feel, but alas I am too shy and frightened of the rejection. A friend suggested a treasure hunt so you can find out in your own way without me being disappointed if you don't feel the same way about me by the end of it. If you decide you would like to be with me, follow the clues to the end, where you will find me waiting and hoping that you make my Christmas wish come true.

You will find the next clue tonight under the brightest star of them all.

With all my love,
Santa x

Lizzy stood astonished at what she had just read — and out loud too! Bob and Claire raised eyebrows at one another, and a few other customers around the room were quietly chattering about the letter.

Lizzy tried to make some sort of sense of the words on the page, but they just swam before her eyes. She had a secret admirer; someone had feelings for her!

Lizzy had never been "lucky in love". She had dated a few men after graduating college, but none had lived up to her secondary school sweetheart who'd broken her heart when they'd separated to go to college at opposite ends of the country.

"Well, where do you think the next clue is hidden then?" Claire enquired, bringing Lizzy out of her reverie.

"Um, I don't know. It says the brightest star. That could be any number of places — the sky is full of them! Besides, it's probably someone messing about. I can't see anyone seriously wanting to declare hidden feelings for me. I mean, who would want a tomboy with unruly curly hair and no fashion sense!"

Lizzy had never been what she would call a "girly girl". Growing up, she had always preferred to play football than with dolls. She stood at five foot six, was slim but not without definition, and had a few light freckles on her cheeks and nose, which she attempted to cover up with foundation and concealer at every opportunity, despite her general dislike of makeup. Without a doubt, Lizzy had very little confidence in her appearance and believed she would still be sitting on the shelf, alone, in her twilight years.

"Lizzy, stop putting yourself down," Claire admonished her. "You have so many good points that you're not seeing. You are kind, thoughtful and caring. You may think your hair is unruly, but I would kill to have your gorgeous curls, and as far as your fashion sense is concerned, there's nothing wrong with casual and comfortable!"

Chuckling to herself, Claire turned to serve another customer while Bob waved goodbye and made his way out of the door to continue on with his post round.

Carefully placing the letter back in the envelope and putting it in her pocket, Lizzy smiled to herself. Perhaps there really was a Santa!

CHAPTER TWO

For the rest of the day, Lizzy's mind was in a misty haze. Not only did she potentially have a secret admirer, but she also had to solve the riddle to find the next clue — if this wasn't a joke of course. By the time the last customers had left the coffee shop, Lizzy was still no nearer to deciphering the mystery.

The bell over the door rang out. Lizzy was about to tell the customer they had just closed for the evening, but upon raising her head from counting the takings in the till, she spotted her oldest friend, Peter Henley.

Peter was six foot tall and well built; as the local handyman, he was used to manual labour and his strong, muscular physique showed as much. His brown hair was swept back in a style Lizzy called "the hand-styled look", which basically meant he had spent all day running his hands through it while he worked. He had the most piercing blue eyes, which always twinkled with a mischievous glint whenever he was around Lizzy. They really were two peas in a pod and had been completely inseparable throughout school, causing havoc wherever they went.

"Oh, hey Pete. Claire has the icing ready in the piping bags out the back! You have sixty Christmas cookies to decorate before the Nativity play starts at seven p.m." Lizzy smirked.

"I don't think so, Lizzy!" Peter chuckled with disbelief. "You and Claire can help me — I'm not doing them on my own!"

"Well, if you want me to ruin them, then I don't mind, but my icing skills are no match for a Henley brother!" Lizzy proclaimed, holding her hands up in surrender.

Upon entering the kitchen, Lizzy and Peter were greeted by a flustered Claire, who was covered from head to toe in icing sugar and edible glitter.

"Great. You can both start decorating the batch on the counter; they've been cooling for a while now." Claire barked her orders like a drill sergeant.

Sensing Claire's stress and knowing there was no appropriate answer other than to pick up an icing bag, Lizzy and Peter rolled their eyes and began to decorate the star-shaped cookies on the workbench.

The three of them worked in silence, Peter and Lizzy pulling faces and throwing edible glitter at each other, attempting to stifle giggles when Claire nearly caught them.

Finally, all sixty cookies were beautifully decorated and boxed up ready to deliver. They all got cleaned up, piled into Claire's delivery van and drove the short distance to the school they had all attended as children.

The school hall had been decorated like a winter wonderland with a Christmas tree in the foyer adorned with white lights, blue ribbon and silver baubles. The stage was set with the Nativity scene. Hay bales were positioned around the manger for Mary, Joseph, the wise men, and the shepherds to sit on. In front of the stage, the choir and narrators took their places on benches, and to the right, the orchestra were setting up their instruments and music stands.

Lizzy and Peter arranged the cookies on a table in the foyer in preparation for the interval while Claire set up the tea urn and coffee machine, along with jugs of squash for the children. Claire turned around just in time to spot Peter sneak a cookie from the table. Realising he had been caught, Peter walked over towards the main hall to take his seat for the start of the performance. As he passed Claire, he winked and grinned.

"Great cookies, Claire. You should go into business!"

Behind him, Lizzy tried unsuccessfully to stifle her laughter as she pushed him past Claire and into the main hall, throwing an apologetic smile to Claire as she went.

Feigning her best annoyed face, Claire followed them to their seats and settled down just in time for the lights to dim and the headmaster to announce the start of the show.

Claire's niece Megan was playing Mary. They watched the performance, smiling, clapping and enjoying every minute. It was a typical school play with rushed lines, mistakes, costume mishaps and at least one instrument out of tune. However, the children were so proud of their little play and, despite the hiccups, it was a humorous but heartfelt performance.

During the interval, the children came running out of the dressing rooms and straight to the refreshment stall.

After an intense few minutes resembling feeding time at the zoo, all that was left were a few cookie crumbs and empty jugs.

Megan and her friend Sally stood talking to Claire. Lizzy overheard the words *letter, star, manger* and *Auntie Lizzy* and realised Claire was telling them about the Secret Santa letter and the treasure hunt. Her eyes darted around the foyer to see if anyone else was listening. Suddenly, something caught her eye, and realisation dawned. The answer to the first clue was right in front of her, hanging above the stage. The star over Bethlehem, directing the wise men to the stable where Jesus was born. Unfortunately, before she could act on her newly garnered information, the headmaster announced the start of the second half. The remaining people in the foyer hurriedly made their way back to their seats before the children returned to the stage.

The second half dragged on for what seemed like hours and all Lizzy could think about was the clue. She knew she had to search the stage after the show.

As soon as the curtain fell, Lizzy was up, out of her seat and heading towards the stage. The way there was like an obstacle course. Lizzy had to manoeuvre through children, parents, musical instruments, stands and seating as the caretaker began stacking the chairs at the side of the hall. Finally reaching the stage, Lizzy climbed the steps and began rummaging amongst the props and scenery. An envelope much like the one she had received earlier was hidden in the straw in the manger. Eagerly, she tore it open and scanned the letter.

My dearest Lizzy,

With only two weeks until Christmas, I am excited for the big day, but my heart is aching for you. I have watched you from afar for many years, but never had the courage to admit my feelings to you.

The fact is, Lizzy, that I love you. I always have and I always will. I hope you can find it in your heart to love me, or let me down gently. Our friendship means too much to me to ruin it by declaring my love, but I have been in the dark for too long. I need to tell you and let this weight be lifted off my shoulders and my heart.

Your next clue will be at a musical scene in the village square.

With all my love,
Santa x

Lizzy's attention was snatched away when she heard Peter calling her from the bottom of the stage steps. Hurriedly, she crammed the letter back into the envelope and went to join him and Claire.

***

Later that evening, Claire, Lizzy and Peter were sitting around the stone fireplace in Claire's living room, drinking hot chocolate and eating Christmas cake, when Claire broke the silence.

"Did you find a clue this evening, Lizzy?"

Cringing on the inside, Lizzy glared at Claire, begging her not to reveal the details to Peter — she knew he'd laugh it off as a joke at her expense. Unfortunately, Claire purposefully ignored the faces Lizzy was making at her as Peter piped up.

"Clue? What do you mean?"

Now Peter's interest had been piqued, there was no point in trying to keep Claire quiet. He'd just coax the information out of her.

Claire proceeded to explain — in too much detail for Lizzy's liking — about the letter, the secret admirer and the clue that should have been solved tonight.

Resigning herself to the inevitable ribbing that would be forthcoming from Peter, Lizzy answered

Claire's question. "Yes, I found another letter in the manger on the stage. It was under the star of Bethlehem," she admitted, pulling the letter from her jeans pocket.

Squealing with excitement, Claire grabbed the letter from Lizzy's hand and read it aloud.

"A musical scene in the village square? That's a bit strange." Claire looked bemused.

"No, that's easy," Peter chimed in. "It's the carol service, surely. Everyone gathers under the Christmas tree to sing carols and raise money for the children's hospital. I have to say that this guy sounds a bit desperate to me! What a sappy way to declare his undying love for you." He wrinkled up his nose with slight disgust.

"Well at least he knows what he wants in life, unlike some people we know!" Lizzy glared pointedly at him. "When are you going to do something with your life? You went travelling after college, but since then, what have you really achieved?"

Rolling his eyes, Peter began the usual speech he had down to a tee for whenever Lizzy quizzed him on his post-college decisions. It had become their standard argument.

"Hey, I *have* started up my own business doing renovation work. I like my life just how it is, thank you, and really, that's all that matters!" Peter fixed his stare on Lizzy, willing her to continue with the argument.

Despite being friends since school, Lizzy and Peter had a heated relationship and knew how to push each other's buttons—which, to the despair of Claire and Peter's brother Mark, happened quite often.

Seeing this could be the start of another fiery debate, Claire jumped into the conversation, reprimanding the pair before Lizzy could retaliate. "Enough, you two. We've had a great evening, let's not spoil it with your bickering!"

Lizzy peered into her hot chocolate, looking sheepish, while Peter smiled apologetically to Claire and continued with the conversation on a much more amicable plane.

"Okay, I give in. It's obviously got you two hooked on love at Christmastime. Look, if you find happiness at the end of this then I'm pleased for you. If you need help finding any clues, let me know." He smiled as he put his used mug in the kitchen sink, slipped his coat on and prepared to go back out into the cold winter night.

Lizzy followed suit and was zipping up her parka when Claire spoke.

"Well, Lizzy, the carol service is tomorrow lunchtime, so as your boss, I am ordering you to have an extended lunch break. You are not to return to work until you have found the next clue!" She hugged both Peter and Lizzy and opened the door.

As she stepped out onto the frosty path, Lizzy paused to wave goodnight to Claire. Turning back around, she realised Peter was already nearly at the front gate.

"Peter, wait!" Lizzy jogged down the path to catch up with him. She linked her arm through his as she fell into step beside him. Receiving a cold shoulder in return, Lizzy gingerly pressed him. "Pete, are you mad at me?"

When she received no response, she continued. "I'm sorry for the harsh things I said to you in there. You know I don't mean them, right? I just want you to be happy and fulfil your dreams. You have so much potential, I don't like seeing you standing still and letting the world and everyone in it flash past your eyes."

Lizzy peered up at him with a look of pure innocence she knew he could never resist.

Huffing out a long breath, Peter looked down at Lizzy. His lip curled as he recognised the "butter wouldn't melt" look in her hazel eyes.

"Okay, you're forgiven. But just so you know, Liz, I am happy. I have a business which is doing great, I live in the village where I grew up with friends and family who love me. What else could a guy ask for?"

"How about someone special to love and share special moments with? To get married, perhaps have children, grow old together?"

"Well, you don't have that either, but you're happy, aren't you?" Peter asked, looking down at Lizzy from his six-foot viewpoint.

With a sigh of resignation, Lizzy voiced her true feelings, those she had only realised herself that afternoon after receiving the Secret Santa letter. "I'm not unhappy, but I feel that I'm ready to find my soulmate. I would love the whole marriage, children, white picket fence one day, but it does feel that life is passing me by. Hopefully my Secret Santa will turn out to be my soulmate, and I can have my fairy tale ending." Lizzy crossed her fingers and looked up to the cold dark sky as if wishing upon a star.

"Well come on, Princess, let me walk you home. We can't have a princess out walking on her own this late now, can we?"

Peter looked serious, but Lizzy knew better. There was a jokey tone to his voice, which was confirmed a minute later when he started chuckling, unable to control the smile bursting onto his lips.

CHAPTER THREE

The next twelve hours flew past and Lizzy found herself standing in the village square surrounded by what seemed like the whole population of the village, all singing along to popular carols and Christmas songs. The decorations committee had outdone themselves this year. Wreaths of pine and holly interspersed with berries, cinnamon sticks and poinsettia hung from every lamp post. In the centre of the square stood the ten-foot Christmas tree, adorned with red ribbons and blue and gold baubles. Underneath the tree, the church choir cheerfully sang a rendition of "God Rest Ye Merry Gentlemen".

Glancing around, Lizzy spotted Bob, the postman, in the crowd. She made her way over to him, thinking that he might recognise the ornate handwriting from the letters.

"Hi Bob, how are you?" Lizzy began, stuttering slightly.

"Hello, Little Lizzy. I'm fine, thanks. Any luck in finding your secret admirer yet?"

"No, I wanted to ask you if you recognised the penmanship from the envelope. It's very unique."

"I'm sorry, but most letters I deliver nowadays have typed address labels, not real handwriting. If I see it again somewhere, I'll be sure to let you know." Bob gave a sympathetic smile.

A little deflated, Lizzy thanked him and excused herself from the conversation. She began roaming around the square looking for the next clue. Engrossed in her mission, she failed to notice the man sitting on a wooden bench at the side of the square.

"Hi, Lizzy. What are you doing here?" the man called out.

Turning, Lizzy met the deep blue eyes she'd wanted to drown in ever since she was a child. For there, sitting on the bench, was her childhood crush, Peter's brother, Mark Henley. Mark was only ten months older than Peter, so they'd been in the same year at school and, for most of their school years, the same class, along with Claire and Lizzy.

"Mark! How are you? I haven't seen you for ages. Peter said you were coming back to spend time with your family over Christmas," Lizzy gushed as she made her way over and gave him a quick hug. When they pulled apart, Mark motioned towards the bench in invitation. Accepting, Lizzy sat down beside him and gazed out at the festivities in the square.

"Well, we Henleys also have to keep up the tradition of winning the gingerbread contest," Mark laughed, knowing full well Lizzy would be on Claire's team and, if the previous years were anything to go by, their main competition.

"Oh, you think you stand a chance, do you?" Lizzy smirked, eyeing Mark surreptitiously. He looked good.

His dark brown hair was a little windswept, but he looked smart as ever in his chinos and jumper. Unfortunately, Mark was doing the same to her, and when their eyes locked, they ended up in a fit of giggles at their childish silliness.

"You haven't told me what you're doing here at the carol service. Shouldn't you be at work, or has Claire turned soft in her old age and started allowing the staff to take lunch breaks?"

The four of them, Mark, Lizzy, Claire and Peter, had been as thick as thieves in secondary school but alas, all headed in different directions once they graduated. Mark had gone to university, qualified as a lawyer and was currently working for a big firm up in the city. He only really came back to the village for the holidays and family get-togethers.

Nodding in agreement and laughing, Lizzy explained about the letter and how she was looking for the next clue.

"Well, if I were you, I'd go and look by the carol singers and the tree first, as that's where the main focus of the celebrations is," Mark suggested.

After hugging Mark goodbye and promising to arrange a catch-up soon, Lizzy stood and walked towards the carollers. Standing in the centre of the square in a red choir gown to match the rest of the choir was Mr Simms, the local vicar, directing the singers in a cheery rendition of "Good King Wenceslas". Lizzy had always thought he looked like one of those Weeble toys of her childhood; he was short and rounded with a joyous personality you couldn't help but smile at.

As Lizzy approached the carollers, he called out to her. "Lizzy, I have something for you!"

She twirled round, slightly taken aback as he handed her a beautifully hand-scripted envelope, the same as the previous clues. Lizzy opened her mouth to enquire who had asked him to pass it on to her, but Mr Simms held up his hand to cut her off.

"I was told to give this to you, but I cannot reveal who asked me. I'm sorry!"

Looking at the letter, Lizzy asked him just one question. "Can you confirm one thing for me please, Mr Simms? Do I know this person?"

A big smile crept onto his features. "Yes, Lizzy. I remember you both as children attending Sunday school and the holiday club during the summer. But then again, pretty much most of the village kids attended those events. You most definitely know your admirer."

"I'm sorry, Mr Simms, how do you know he is an admirer?" Lizzy gingerly enquired.

Smiling knowingly, Mr Simms clapped Lizzy on the shoulder. "I have had many a conversation with the author over the years about his feelings towards you. He struggled with his feelings for quite some time and eventually came to me asking for advice. Unfortunately, he did not heed my advice, as that was over ten years ago now and he's only just acting on it."

Shocked that Mr Simms had known about this secret admirer for such a long time, Lizzy stared blankly at the letter, running her thumb over the red wax securing the flap.

Mr Simms made a suggestion. "My dear, don't forget, as I have offered in the past to all of you young ones, if you ever need to discuss anything, the vicarage door is always open and I can usually guarantee that Mrs Simms will have a pot of fresh tea on the go and a cake fresh out of the oven."

After thanking him for his honesty and kind words, Lizzy left him to continue conducting the choir. She found a quiet bench to sit on and read the next letter.

My dearest Lizzy,

I suppose I should begin to give you some information about myself. You have known me since year one at school and I have loved you since that first day when Jeremy Smith was told off for pinching Claire's arm and you comforted her, trying to stop her crying.

From that day, I knew you were warm and kind and I wanted nothing more than to be your friend and make you happy. I hope over the years I have achieved this goal, because you deserve the best in life.

You will find the next clue somewhere warm and cosy. Keep your eyes peeled, as it will appear as if by magic!

With all my love,
Santa x

Lizzy studied the letter again and again. So the list of potential admirers had been narrowed down to approximately ten people. If only she could remember all the boys from her year one class. However, she knew that, as the head of the social committee in school and the local hub of information, Claire would be sure to name all of them and most probably know intricate details such as their current whereabouts, marital status and inside leg measurements.

If she wanted to crack the mystery that was Santa, Lizzy realised, she needed to have a long discussion with Claire.

***

Returning to work after lunch, Lizzy met Claire's eager look of interest with a wave of her hand and marched through the shop into the kitchen to hang up her coat. An overly excited Claire followed her into the kitchen, not prepared to be ignored.

"Well, did you find another clue?"

Knowing how persistent Claire would be if she didn't spill the information immediately, Lizzy pulled the letter out of her back pocket and held it out. Once she'd read it, Claire nodded, returned the letter to the envelope and handed it back.

"We'll sit down tonight and make a list of the possible culprits," she announced as if she was in an Agatha Christie murder mystery.

Rolling her eyes, Lizzy put the letter back in her pocket and returned to the front room to collect the dirty dishes and serve the next customers.

CHAPTER FOUR

Later that evening, once the last customer had left, Claire turned the door sign round to "Closed" and helped Lizzy take the last of the washing up through to the kitchen. They returned with two large mugs of hot chocolate and a plate of sandwiches and sat down in the nook by the fireplace.

Throwing another log into the fire and watching the flames lick the edges as it began to catch alight, Lizzy reeled off the names of the boys she could remember from their class while Claire wrote them down on the back of the letter.

Jeremy Smith
Peter Henley
Mark Henley
James Cartwright
Steven Ball
Andrew Forbes
Lucas Mills

Bryan Durrant
Sam Anderson
Liam Fowler

"Okay, we'll go through the list one by one," said Claire. "I think we have all of them. At least, I don't recall anyone else in our class."

"Well, Jeremy is mentioned in the letter so it can't be him, and I know Steven is married with children," Lizzy pondered.

"Andrew is engaged to Sally Green from the bank, and I'm quite sure Lucas announced he is gay a few years back," Claire added. The conversation veered off subject slightly when she started giggling. "Oh my, do you remember when we all had that snowball fight in the park and Emma Tucker threw the snowball that smacked Sam right in the face? That was the beginning of the annual boys versus girls snowball wars. Mmm, I'll have to ask Megan if they still have that tradition."

Claire began to reminisce about other events and tales from their childhood involving the possible suspects. Little did they realise how the time flew, until Lizzy couldn't contain a yawn anymore.

She brought the conversation back on track. "So that leaves us with James, Peter, Mark, Bryan, Liam and Sam."

From out of nowhere, the tall oak grandfather clock in the corner chimed midnight. Lizzy and Claire stared at it in disbelief. Had they really been reminiscing and discussing these men for over five hours?

Deciding it was time to make a move, Lizzy and Claire gathered up the mugs and dishes they had been using and loaded them into the kitchen dishwasher.

"Can you dampen down the fire in the grate, please?" Claire called from the kitchen as Lizzy returned to the nook to put on her coat.

The fire was almost down to the embers already, but Lizzy poked around the charred remains and threw a shovelful of sand over them just to be sure. Determining the fire would not re-light again overnight, she returned the shovel to the ash bucket beside the hearth and resolved to clear the grate of the cold ash in the morning. It was then that something strange caught her eye. There, hanging from the mantle, was a small red and green stocking with her name delicately embroidered around the felt turnover in gold thread. Gingerly, Lizzy removed the stocking and peered inside. There it was, the next clue, along with a charming, hand-painted Christmas bauble depicting a winter scene of a pond with ice skaters.

When Claire returned to the main room to see Lizzy holding the stocking and bauble, she was taken aback.

"Where did that appear from?" she asked, slightly creeped out that someone had been in the shop whilst they were cleaning up in the kitchen.

"It was hanging from the mantle." Lizzy tore open the envelope to reveal another beautifully written note.

My dearest Lizzy,

Do you remember skating on the pond with me all those many years ago? I used to be in awe of your ability to glide over the ice like a princess. I was good, but nowhere near your standard.

By now you have probably narrowed down your list of possible suspects. Please don't worry too much, I am determined to declare myself to you. You will find me on Christmas Eve giving gifts out to the local children and listening to everyone's wishes for the holiday season.

The next clue will be found where the lights shine brightly for all to see.

With all my love,
Santa x

"Ooh, the plot thickens!" Claire giggled. "Who used to ice skate with you on the pond? Anyone on the list?"

"Um, let me see the list." Lizzy took the piece of paper from Claire. "I don't recall Sam ever skating. Liam and James did. Mark and Peter were always on the ice, and Bryan was more into football than skating, so he never joined us."

"Okay, so we've narrowed the list further. Liam, James, Peter and Mark are our prime suspects," Claire announced as she drew a line through Sam and Bryan's names. "Who do you want it to be?"

That was the question that Lizzy had been pondering, but she didn't want to admit her hopes and wishes just yet. After all, Santa could turn out to be someone completely different.

"I haven't really thought about it. It all still seems so surreal."

Seeing Claire about to probe her for more details, Lizzy briskly changed the subject to one she knew Claire couldn't argue with. "Now I must get home to bed if you want me to open up the shop tomorrow."

Smiling at having successfully side-stepped the question, Lizzy waved goodnight to Claire. She got into her cold car and shivered until the heater finally warmed up. Unfortunately for her, this was as she pulled onto her driveway.

***

Crawling under the duvet that night, Lizzy couldn't help but ponder the options.

Possibility number one was Liam. He was a nice enough guy and Lizzy had always got on well with him, but he had never entered her thoughts as potential boyfriend material. Although, she wasn't completely against the idea.

Possibility number two was James, whom she had dated through the last two years of secondary school. They had broken up when they'd left to go to college. Lizzy had put on a brave face at the time, but the break-up had shaken her to the core. James had been her first real boyfriend, and it had taken months to get over the pain and heartbreak. If Lizzy was being honest with herself, her subconscious was telling her that Santa was likely to be James. She had seen him a few times when he stopped by the tearoom for a cup of coffee, and he always had a sombre look on his face. Could he still be in love with her after all these years?

Possibility number three was Peter. Since she could remember, she and Peter had been best friends. They looked out for each other and had each other's backs. After Lizzy's last relationship had ended dismally, Peter had brought the tub of ice cream round and sat with her for hours as she sobbed on his shoulder. No, Peter was her friend, he didn't have feelings for her. He couldn't be Santa.

Then came possibility number four: Mark. It was no surprise to Lizzy that she secretly wished Santa was Mark. She'd had a crush on him since junior school that had only intensified the older they got. After the discussion on the bench today, she hoped Mark was Santa. The way he held her gaze with his ocean blue eyes and smiled at her still made her weak at the knees.

Turning out the bedside lamp, Lizzy drifted off to sleep, dreaming happily of Santa and Mark.

CHAPTER FIVE

Lizzy woke to a bright light streaming in through the bedroom window. She jumped out of bed, ran downstairs and out onto the front porch to witness the first flurries of snow that winter.

A blue pick-up truck pulled up outside the front gate. Peter jumped out wearing his trademark jeans, flannel dress shirt over a tight-fitting T-shirt, and a sheepskin-lined jacket and boots. He strolled up the garden path, his face dropping as he realised what Lizzy was wearing.

"Are you insane? You'll catch your death out here wearing those pyjamas!" Peter turned her around by her shoulders and pushed her back into the warmth of the house.

"Hey, good morning to you too!" Lizzy said sarcastically.

Heading straight to the kitchen to turn on the coffee maker, Peter spotted the letters on the counter and frowned. "Have you had more letters from the weird Santa Stalker?"

"He's not weird or a stalker, he's a hopeless romantic who apparently loves me. You know, it is possible for someone to like me like that!" Lizzy went on the attack, lightly smacking Peter's arm in annoyance.

"Hey, I know you're God's gift to all men, but you're not my type, sorry!" Peter said. "So when will Santa reveal himself to you? Quite a lot of the village are keen to find out who the mystery man is."

"He'll be dressed as Santa, handing out presents on Christmas Eve to the children and listening to their Christmas wishes."

"Getting close, then. Christmas Eve is a week today," Peter said, counting the days on his fingers.

"I know. Part of me can't wait to find out who it is, and the other part doesn't want the day to arrive, just in case it's someone I really don't like," Lizzy admitted, biting her bottom lip.

"Well, there's no point fretting over it. What will be will be. Now, do you want a lift to work so you haven't got to drive in the snow?"

"Yes please. I'll just get showered and change and I'll be right down. Help yourself to breakfast!" Lizzy called as she ran up the stairs, knowing full well that she didn't need to offer; he already had the fridge open and had begun to prepare breakfast for the both of them.

***

"Thanks for dropping me at work. I hate driving in the snow!" Lizzy said as Peter pulled up. Glancing out of the side window, Lizzy was surprised to see Claire standing inside the shop doorway, talking to Liam Fowler.

Lizzy hopped down from the truck and turned back to Peter.

"I'll come by and pick you up at seven to go to the tree lighting ceremony, if you want?" Peter suggested. "Unless of course you already have plans for this evening?"

"No, that'll be great, thanks. You can give me a hand to find the next Santa clue. It's going to be hidden under the tree somewhere." Lizzy beamed, knowing that the mere subject of Secret Santa was enough to get Peter's eyes rolling.

Smirking at his reaction, Lizzy waved as she slammed the truck door shut and hurried into the coffee shop, out of the cold.

"Morning, Claire. Hi, Liam, how are you?" she asked.

"Hi, Lizzy. Liam here is trying to persuade me to upgrade the computer system so we can link it to the till and we'll no longer need to run the end of the month reports, it'll do it for us!" Claire explained with a look of "Help! Save me!", which she successfully hid from Liam.

"Yes, Lizzy, you have to talk Claire into going with the new modern package. It'll save you so much time and money in the long run," Liam was on his hard sell. After school, he had studied business at university and had recently been headhunted by a top computer software company as their number one sales representative.

"It sounds wonderful, it really does," Claire said, "but the fact of the matter is that we run a coffee shop, not a high-end restaurant. It takes us less than a couple of minutes each evening to count the takings, and half an hour to run the end of month reports for the accountant. Our revenue can't justify this fancy system. I'm sorry!"

"Not to worry. I wouldn't be a good salesman if I didn't try!" Liam smiled, albeit sadly.

Giving him a sympathetic smile, Lizzy went round the counter to pour him a coffee.

"So how's your new job going? Are you enjoying it?" she enquired, trying to pull Liam out of his mood.

"It's slow going, but I enjoy being my own boss. I just have to log my sales once a week with the head office. It enables me to be around in case there's an emergency with my mum." Liam smiled in thanks as he accepted the coffee from Lizzy.

"Oh, yes, how is your mum now? Claire mentioned she was in a car accident and was in hospital for a while."

"She's home now, but she broke her arm and her ankle, so she relies on me and my sister to help her get around, do chores and run errands for her. Hopefully, she'll be out of the plaster casts in a few weeks."

"Oh gosh. Well, I hope she has a speedy recovery, and if you ever need any help with anything, just give me a call."

Handing over the money for the coffee, Liam thanked Lizzy and excused himself, having to get back to work.

***

The rest of the day flew by in a blur. The lunchtime rush was a nightmare as usual, and Claire and Lizzy were relieved when the grandfather clock in the corner chimed seven o'clock and they could turn the door sign to "Closed".

"What a day!" Claire moaned as she slumped into the nearest chair. "I didn't think it would end!"

"Jeez, I can't believe how fussy that lady from the craft shop was about her cup of coffee!" Lizzy exclaimed in disbelief. "I mean, if she wants soya milk, low fat, with a caramel shot, poured into a hip flask, she needs to go to a fancy barista shop, not the local tearoom."

Giggling at the memory, Claire chimed into Lizzy's rant. "Did you see the look on her face, though, when Mrs Pinkerton from the library tutted and suggested she should move to the city if that was to be her daily coffee order, as no one wants to wait in line for ten minutes while we faff about making it?"

"I wish I'd had my camera on me. The number of people who complain about her attitude when she's serving her customers, they would love to see her put in her place." Changing the subject, Lizzy asked, "Are you going to the tree lighting ceremony tonight?"

"Honestly, I don't think I will. I just want to go home, take a long soak in the bath and curl up in bed with a good book," Claire mused dreamily.

Throwing Claire a sympathetic smile, Lizzy began cashing up. When the bell above the door chimed, she looked up and smiled and waved at Peter.

"Hiya! I'll be five minutes, do you mind waiting for me?" she said, putting the takings in the safe and closing down the till system.

"No, of course not, provided you allow me to sample one of those delicious-looking donuts you have in the display case!" Peter pouted, but Lizzy was not buying it — she could see the wicked glint in his eyes.

Still, she handed one of the donuts over to Peter, rolling her eyes at Claire, who was giggling at the interaction.

"Peter, you're insufferable," Lizzy said with mock annoyance. "Every time you come in here, you leave with something you haven't paid for!"

"Oh, but Lizzy, how can you resist feeding this poor, hungry face? You don't want me wasting away now do you?" Peter dipped his head and peered at Lizzy through his eyelashes, giving her his best puppy dog eyes.

"Grrr, you… I… Grrr!" Lizzy tried and failed to give Peter a stern look, but he could tell that she wanted to burst into laughter. Instead, she turned on her heel and marched into the kitchen, leaving Peter and Claire erupting in a fit of giggles.

True to her word, Lizzy was ready in five minutes. Claire ushered them out of the shop, saying she would finish locking up so they could reach the village square in time for the tree lighting.

The night was cold with a biting wind that whipped around their ankles. Wrapped up in coats, gloves and woolly hats, Peter and Lizzy strolled through the streets towards the village square, following the sound of Christmas music being played over the public address system. Most of the shops and houses en route already had their trees, fairy lights and holiday decorations on display, giving the cold streets a warm, homely feel.

Glancing sideways at Peter, Lizzy couldn't put her finger on it but knew that something was wrong. He seemed to be struggling with something internally. A few times, she'd noticed him turn to say something to her then stop himself as if unsure how to put it into words. Figuring he'd eventually start talking, Lizzy kept quiet and let him sort through his thoughts.

Finally, he broke the silence. "So, did you say there would be another clue hidden somewhere at the ceremony tonight?"

"Yes, apparently it will be under the tree. I know you think it's silly, but will you please help me find it?"

"Look, Lizzy," Peter said, taking her by the shoulders and looking her straight in the eye. "Yes, I think it's a cowardly way to tell you that he loves you, and in some ways it's cruel on you to drag it out for so long. It must be hard for him, too, not knowing if he's doing it all for nothing. I know it means a lot to you to find out who this guy is, and as your friend, I will support you with whatever you need."

Understanding the genuine concern he felt for her, Lizzy smiled in appreciation, grabbed Peter's arm and threaded her own through it. "Thank you, Pete. It does mean a lot to me, and I understand your feelings on the subject, but I'll be careful, I promise."

They reached the village square with minutes to spare. Small bonfires were lit in each corner, and market stalls sold hot chocolate, mulled wine, decorations and other Christmas gifts and paraphernalia. Christmas tunes rang out from the public address system, cutting through the crisp night air and the chattering from the crowd that had gathered around the tree to await the beginning of the ceremony.

After a few words from the mayor, a group of local school children pulled the lever to light the Christmas tree. The crowd cheered and clapped as, row by row, the lights lit the tree, shining brightly across the square. As the crowd started to mingle and chat, Lizzy and Peter made a beeline towards the tree. Peeking out from under the red and white felt skirt that covered the tree stand, Lizzy found the next letter.

"I've found it!" Lizzy called to Peter, who was elbow-deep in the bottom branches around the other side, fighting with a particularly uncooperative length of tinsel.

Managing to free himself, Peter joined Lizzy and read the letter over her shoulder.

My dearest Lizzy,
I still can't believe I have taken the plunge and am admitting my feelings for you. I will admit that I'm terrified I am doing the wrong thing in coming clean after all this time.
I used to sit in maths, pretending to pay attention to Miss Lewings, but fractions and algebra couldn't distract me from

the concentration on your face, the slight wrinkling of your nose as you frowned, trying to understand the formulas. I suppose you are part of the reason I didn't do brilliantly at school; you were too much of a distraction for me.

The next clue will be found under the trophy.

All my love,

Santa x

Looking up at Peter, Lizzy was puzzled. "Who was in Miss Lewings' maths class with us?"

"Erm, I can't rightly remember everyone, but I remember I used to sit with James. We hardly got any work done, we spent too much time passing notes and drawing caricatures of Miss Lewings."

Frowning in disapproval, Lizzy played the letter over in her head as they walked back to Peter's truck parked outside the coffee shop.

***

As they pulled up outside Lizzy's house, Peter's face turned from jokey to deadly serious.

"Lizzy, I have something I must declare to you. I can't be your friend anymore!"

The blood drained from Lizzy's face as she wondered if she was hallucinating. Had Peter really just ended their friendship?

Realising how his declaration was affecting Lizzy, he jumped in to clarify what he meant, taking her hands in his. "Lizzy! Don't look so worried. I only meant tomorrow during the gingerbread contest! You and Claire are mine and Mark's biggest competition!"

"Oh, Peter! Don't do that to me!" Lizzy cried, the relief evident on her face.

Grinning, Peter dropped a kiss on her forehead. "Sorry to scare you, but don't worry—after we wipe the floor with you tomorrow, you and Claire are more than welcome to join me and Mark in our celebration dinner at Fernando's!"

"Huh, dream on, Peter Henley. You and your brother are going down tomorrow!" Lizzy pushed open the truck door and jumped out. As she shut the door behind her, Peter wound down the window.

"Well, I guess we'll have to see then, Miss Chesterfield! May the best team win!"

With a grin at Peter, Lizzy walked up her front path. She turned to wave, then opened the front door and entered the dark house.

CHAPTER SIX

"So, Lizzy, we have to be at the community centre by twelve to set up our kitchen area," Claire called from the kitchen of the coffee shop.

Due to the prestigious Annual Gingerbread Contest that afternoon, all the local shops were closing early.

"I've gathered up all the decorating tools — can you grab the packs of sweets from the pantry please?" Lizzy called back.

At 11:45 a.m., Claire and Lizzy pulled into the community centre car park, just as Peter and Mark took the space next to them. All four got out of the vehicles, completely ignoring each other, and began unloading the equipment from their boots.

Unfortunately, Claire and Lizzy's kitchen area was next to Mark and Peter's, which meant jokey insults would probably be thrown throughout the four hours they had to produce a gingerbread house stunning enough to impress the judges.

At twelve, the mayor climbed up onto the stage to announce the start of the competition and read the rules to the contestants.

"The contestants are competing for this: the Gingerbread Trophy!" The mayor held up the small token trophy.

"Claire, that's it!" Lizzy whispered. "The letter said the next clue would be under the trophy. That must be the trophy!"

But as the mayor placed the trophy back down on the lectern, she could see that there was nothing underneath it.

As soon as the whistle blew, each of the eight teams started bustling around their kitchens, mixing, crushing, icing, and sticking sweets and gingerbread together. Lizzy looked around, trying to get a feel for the competition. Apart from herself and Claire, Peter and Mark, there were only two other people Lizzy knew: James Cartwright and Jessica Strong. Her eyes caught James's and she smiled and waved. She hadn't seen him for a couple of months, and she wasn't going to admit it, but she felt the old pull on the heartstrings she always did when he was in the same room as her. She was still attracted to him, and that thought unsettled her somewhat.

Around the halfway point, Lizzy raised her head to peer over at the Henley brothers' progress. Something didn't seem right; Mark was looking flustered and Peter's scowl could sour milk. Listening carefully whilst pretending to wash a mixing bowl, Lizzy could hear the agitated whispers between the boys.

"Why did you think it would be a great idea to add fruit into the biscuit mix?" Peter demanded.

"Look, I'm sorry, but I read that it gives the biscuit an extra flavour that no one else would have," Mark said, giving him a sideways glance.

"Yeah, well, thanks to your bright idea, the biscuit won't stand up on its own because it's too soft, which means that we can't build a house, which — as you may not have realised — is the whole point of the competition!" Peter's voice grew more and more raised as he ranted, to the extent that many of the other contestants were looking over to see what the commotion was about.

Realising the scene he was creating, Peter threw down his oven gloves, muttered, "I'm going to get some air!" and stormed out of the hall, leaving Mark staring sorrowfully after him.

"I'm just going to check on Peter," Lizzy told Claire as she grabbed her coat and Peter's from the coat hooks. She gave Mark a sympathetic smile on her way past and walked out into the chilly air of the car park. Peter was sitting on the curb with his head in his hands.

"That sky looks like we will have a snowfall any minute now. You'd better put your coat on; we don't want you ill for Christmas." Lizzy sat down beside him and nudged his shoulder with her own. "Are you okay? What happened in there?"

"Mark is a complete idiot! He's ruined our chances of winning the trophy with his crazy idea of adding fruit to the biscuits," Peter explained, anger leaching through his words.

"So you can't build a house, but I bet it'll taste good!" Lizzy attempted to lighten Peter's mood.

"I was quite harsh with him, wasn't I?"

"Yes. By the stricken look on his face as I followed you out here, I would say he's very sorry for the mistake and has absolutely no idea how to make amends. Now, how about we go back inside in the warm and try to make good your flat-pack house?"

Turning towards her with a disbelieving look on his face, Peter couldn't help but chuckle. "Okay, come on, I've got some grovelling to do. Oh, and this doesn't mean we're friends again, by the way!" He grinned at Lizzy as he put an arm around her shoulders and guided her back into the hall.

By the end of the four hours, Lizzy and Claire had produced a beautifully crafted gingerbread house with boiled-sweet stained-glass windows, crushed peppermints as snow and enough sweets to give any dentist a heart attack.

Mark and Peter had apologised to each other and managed to produce a house that was heavily propped up on the inside with candy canes and piles of boiled sweets—which mysteriously appeared on their counter after Lizzy had asked to borrow a sieve.

The judging panel, made up of the mayor, his wife and the cookery teacher from the secondary school, made their way around the stands taking notes on presentation, decoration, taste and originality. After a short intermission, the mayor climbed up on the stage and addressed the crowd of eagerly waiting villagers and contestants.

"Ladies, gentlemen and children, it with great pleasure that I announce the results of this year's gingerbread contest. Well done to all the teams—you have produced amazing creations, and I can say with a degree of certainty that everyone in the room cannot wait for the opportunity to taste them.

"Therefore, without further ado, the winners of the Annual Gingerbread Contest are Claire and Lizzy from the Wooden Spoon Coffee Shop. Congratulations to you both! Please come up and collect your trophy."

Gushing at the applause, Claire and Lizzy ascended the steps onto the stage. As the mayor held out the trophy to Claire, who accepted it with a beaming smile, Lizzy spotted one of Santa's beautifully decorated envelopes on the lectern. It hadn't been there at the beginning of the competition, which could only mean one thing: Santa had been — and perhaps still was — in the room.

Forgetting the hubbub and applause around her, Lizzy picked up the envelope. Running her hand over the embossed writing and the wax seal, she smiled as she followed Claire back down the steps to the kitchen area.

"Well done, you two!" James said as he approached their counter.

"Why, thank you, James," Claire replied cheerfully. "How are you? We haven't seen you in the coffee shop for a while; what have you been up to?"

"I went travelling around Europe for three months. It was wonderful. If you're interested, I have loads of photos and stories about my travels — perhaps we can all catch up at some point in the near future?" James suggested, looking longingly at Lizzy, who just stood transfixed, unable to speak.

Claire, noticing the looks between Lizzy and James, cleared her throat and made excuses for them to leave but assured James that they would be in touch to arrange a date for catch-up drinks.

"What do you think you're doing?" she asked Lizzy, once they were gone. "You cannot be serious, looking at James like that after the way you two ended it. He made you miserable — it took me and Peter months to get the old Lizzy back! Please tell me you're not considering trying again."

"What? No, of course not, don't be silly." Lizzy hated lying to Claire, but the stern look she was receiving was definitely not one she wanted to anger further with the revelation that she wished either Mark or James was Santa.

***

Fernando's was a newly opened Italian restaurant on the high street. It was decorated in a Mediterranean style, with light, earthy colours, a tiled floor and olive trees growing in terracotta pots dotted around the room. Lizzy and Claire were thoroughly enjoying rubbing Mark and Peter's noses in their victory by having the trophy as the table centrepiece during the whole meal.

"The best team won, so congratulations, and I genuinely do mean that," Peter said, laughing at the shocked look from both Claire and Lizzy.

The conversation flowed smoothly, and it was almost as if the years since secondary school hadn't flown by. Raising his glass, Mark toasted Claire and Lizzy and their triumph. They all raised their glasses in agreement.

It was the sound of the waiter stacking chairs on top of a nearby table that alerted the four to the lateness of the hour. After paying the bill and leaving a tip, they donned their outdoor clothing and ventured out into the cold, deserted street. They bid farewell to each other, with Claire agreeing to drop Mark back at his parents' place as it was just round the corner from her house, while Peter would drive Lizzy home.

Peter rushed to get into the cab of his truck, turning over the engine to start the heater and warm up before pulling out into the road.

"Have you received another clue today?" he asked, glancing over at Lizzy.

"Oh yes—I completely forgot about it!" Lizzy pulled the envelope from her back pocket.

Carefully, she opened it and read the letter out loud.

My dearest Lizzy,

We have grown up so much over the years. Some of us have moved away, some moved back to the village. I can tell you now with certainty that whenever I am apart from you, my heart aches and I feel like a part of me is missing. I hope

at the end of this adventure, you will find it in your heart to
make me whole again.

The next clue will be hidden behind a door.
All my love,
Santa x

"Oh please!" Peter scoffed. "It's almost sickening, the way this guy is drooling all over you, and you have no idea who he is. It's creepy!"

Staring at the magical penmanship, Lizzy spoke softly. "It's not creepy, I think it's sweet. Can you imagine how he's felt all these years with this secret bottled up, scared of admitting his feelings? He's finally gathered up the courage to tell me how he feels. I just hope that it's who I think it is and we can be happy together. I don't want to disappoint him."

Raising his eyebrows, surprised and intrigued, Peter pushed Lizzy for answers. "So, who do you want it to be then?" he enquired as he pulled into Lizzy's driveway behind her car.

With a blush growing from ear to ear, Lizzy said, "No one, I haven't really thought about it. So anyway, thank you for the lift. I better be heading in; I've got to get up early in the morning." Lizzy smiled, too cheerfully, as she exited the car.

Before Peter had a chance to roll down his window and respond to her, she had reached the house, turned, waved and was heading inside.

"Don't think you've got away without confessing, Little Lizzy! I will eke the truth out of you!"

Peter's lip curled up in a smirk as he reversed out of the driveway and drove off home.

Chapter Seven

The lunchtime rush was finally over when Bob, the postman, walked into the coffee shop and perched on one of the counter stools.

"Afternoon, ladies. Well done on the gingerbread contest win yesterday. I bet the Henley brothers were spitting feathers by the end!" he chuckled.

"They certainly weren't happy, but it's just a bit of fun—nothing too serious really! We were all still talking to each other afterwards," Claire replied from behind the counter.

"Can I get a cup of tea please, Lizzy? Milk and two sugars," Bob requested.

"Certainly, Bob. Would you like a mince pie too? They're fresh out of the oven, still warm!" Lizzy proffered the plate of mince pies.

"Ooh, they smell divine, I couldn't possible say no. Thank you." Bob grinned and took a bite from the pie he had selected.

"Your round must take double the time during the Christmas season, what with all the cards and parcels being sent in the mail." Lizzy chatted merrily to Bob while he enjoyed his tea and pie.

"Yes, it does. However, it's nice to see the smiles on everyone's faces when they receive a package from a friend or relative they haven't seen for a while.

"Well, I must dash. I have a few more deliveries to make then I have to go and feed the Fowlers' cat while they're away visiting relatives for the holiday period," Bob stated as he wrapped up warm against the elements in his Royal Mail regulation coat, hat and gloves. "Thank you for the tea and pie—see you tomorrow!" He waved as he left the shop.

Realising what Bob had just let slip, Lizzy darted from around the counter and went rushing out into the street, calling after him.

"Bob, wait!"

Bob turned, a little startled.

"What did you say about the Fowlers? Have they gone away? All of them, even Liam?"

"Yes, the whole family has gone to Liam's grandmother's in Ireland for Christmas. They left two days ago. I agreed to feed Mr Tibbs, their cat, while they're away. He's such a sweet little fluffball, so affectionate."

Not overly interested in Bob's friendship with the Fowlers' cat, Lizzy thanked him for his help and excused herself, stating she should get back in the warm.

Claire frowned when she walked back in. "Where did you run off to?"

"Sorry, it was just something Bob said about feeding the Fowlers' cat," Lizzy explained. "If Liam's out of the country visiting relatives, then he couldn't have been at the gingerbread contest yesterday."

"Well, yes, that's right, but why should he have been at the contest?" Claire looked puzzled.

Lizzy shook her head. "No—don't you understand? Santa had to be at the contest yesterday. The letter was nowhere in sight at the beginning, but it was under the trophy at the end. Santa had to have put it there during the contest. He was in the room!" She spelled it out to Claire, who looked like she was slowly grasping Lizzy's meaning.

"Ah, so if Liam was away, then he can't have been at the contest and is therefore not Santa," Claire finished for Lizzy, nodding in understanding. "So, who does that leave you with now then?"

"I've whittled the list down to three possibilities: Mark, Peter or James."

"How do you feel about James potentially being Santa?"

"Honestly, I don't really know. When I saw him the other day, I could feel twinges of the old feelings, but then I remembered how upset I was when we broke up. I don't think I could go through something like that again if it didn't work out," Lizzy mused, unable to make eye contact. She began to play with the corner of her apron. "I think it would be great to start with, like any new relationship, but I don't think I would be able to completely bury the past, so it might not be a great idea."

Draping her arm across Lizzy's shoulders, Claire brought her in for a sideways hug. "Well, whoever it is, and whether you decide to make a go of it with them or not, you've always got me and Peter to fall back on if you need us. Peter brings the ice cream; I bring the spoons!"

Lizzy couldn't help but giggle at that, remembering how the pair had appeared on her doorstep, enveloped her in a group hug and brought her out of the doldrums after her break-up with James.

Smiling with appreciation for her friend, Lizzy went about clearing a recently vacated table of crockery and cutlery.

"Hey, Claire, is it still okay for me to leave early tomorrow so I can go and pick out a Christmas tree?" she called as she made her way into the kitchen to load the dirty plates into the dishwasher.

"Yes, of course, but how are you going to get it home?" Claire asked. "You won't be able to carry it in the house by yourself."

"I hadn't thought that far ahead!" Lizzy sighed, reaching for her phone.

She punched a few numbers in and waited while the call connected and the dial tone was replaced by Peter's voice.

"Hey Liz. What's up, everything okay?"

"Yeah, fine, thanks, but I was wondering if I can ask a favour? Would you be able to meet me tomorrow at the Christmas tree farm and help me get a tree back home please?" Lizzy asked, with a pleading tone to her voice that she knew Peter couldn't resist.

"Yeah, sure. What time do you want to meet?"

Lizzy discussed the details with Peter then hung up, satisfied that her problem had been solved.

"Brilliant. Tomorrow's sorted," she explained to Claire. "Peter is going to meet me at the Christmas tree farm, and we can load it onto the back of his truck."

"Great. I have to get my tree at some point too, I keep forgetting it." Changing tack slightly, Claire broached the subject of Secret Santa. "Have you worked out the next clue yet? What did it say again?"

"No, not yet. It said the next clue would be hidden behind a door. That could mean any door, and in this village, there are hundreds of them. It could be anywhere!" Lizzy proclaimed, slightly annoyed.

"Well, Santa hasn't been too cruel in hiding his clues so far, so I think the answer will come to you, just like it did with the trophy at the gingerbread contest." Claire tried to reassure her, knowing Lizzy wouldn't rest until she found the next clue.

***

The rest of the afternoon flew by, and at seven p.m. Claire and Lizzy shut the door after the last customer and got to work cleaning up and preparing the shop for the next day, stacking the chairs, sweeping the floors, wiping down the counters and tables and restocking the fridges and display cabinets with fresh pastries and sandwiches.

After bidding farewell to Claire and locking the front door, Lizzy got into her car and drove home. She pulled into the driveway and turned off the engine, then climbed the steps to the front porch. In the summer she would sit on the little porch swing and watch the world go by, not that much went by in the little country lane she lived down. With a cool glass of lemonade, she'd watch the sun set behind the trees, leaving a golden haze on the horizon which slowly faded to black. Glancing at the swing, Lizzy was surprised to see a gift-wrapped box sitting on the seat. She picked it up and examined it, but found no notes, just a gift tag with her name on it.

She opened the front door and walked in, placing the box on the kitchen counter before removing her hat, scarf, coat and boots. Checking the box out the corner of her eye, Lizzy filled the kettle and set it to boil for a cup of tea.

Gingerly, Lizzy picked up the box and sat down on a bar stool at the kitchen counter. She removed the gift tag and carefully examined the writing on it. She had seen it before, but where?

Unwrapping the bright silver and blue wrapping paper and ribbons, Lizzy revealed an ornate wooden advent calendar along with a note.

Sorry this gift is late; it took longer than expected to finish it. Please skip forward to today's door. I promise there are sweets in all the other doors, so you won't miss out on the treats.

Still not quite putting a name to the handwriting, Lizzy opened the door for the eighteenth. Inside was a beautiful heart-shaped charm on a silver bracelet, and another letter.

My dearest Lizzy,

So, you probably need to know a little bit more about me. You already know a lot from just being friends for so long. However, there are some aspects of me that no one knows.

1. *I am scared of heights. Even going up ladders gives me the shakes*
2. *I am a closet romantic (but you have probably already guessed that from these letters)*
3. *I took a course in calligraphy and creative writing at college*

I will tell you more in the next clue, which you will find by using an axe. By the way, this calendar will keep adding to your charm bracelet between now and Christmas to hopefully help reveal my true identity.

All my love,

Santa x

Lizzy was stunned. She re-read the letter and the note, trying to place the handwriting, but failing miserably. She took the charm bracelet out of its box and fastened it around her wrist. She had wanted a charm bracelet since she was a little girl, but despite always being on her Christmas wish list, she'd never received one. Smiling, she got up to pour her cup of tea. Could it be a coincidence that Santa had given her a charm brace-let, or did he know her Christmas wish from childhood?

Examining the bracelet, Lizzy pondered the last week and how just a few letters could potentially change her life. She wouldn't admit it to Peter and Claire, but she felt lonely at times. Even when they were together chatting, eating a meal or watching a film, she felt like something was missing. Hopefully the author of the letters would turn out to be the missing piece of the jigsaw puzzle of her heart.

CHAPTER EIGHT

The next morning met Lizzy with dark clouds and the sound of rain hitting the pane of her bedroom window. She found the sound mesmerising. It gave her a sense of calm looking ahead to the busy week before Christmas.

Today was going to be hectic. Claire had nominated Lizzy as chief baker to produce two hundred Christmas cookies to serve to the spectators of the local dance school's rendition of *The Nutcracker*, which was being performed the following day.

Grumbling as she freed her feet from the tangle of covers and blankets, Lizzy rolled out of bed and began her morning routine. She was about to grab her coat and pull on her boots when she spotted the advent calendar sitting on the kitchen counter. Eager to see the next clue, Lizzy opened the day's door to find another charm to add to her bracelet. This time it was a delicate yellow rose. The brief note attached read:

My dearest Lizzy,
This yellow rose is a symbol of our friendship. I hope that
whatever happens between us, we can always remain friends.
All my love,
Santa x

Smiling, Lizzy added the rose to her bracelet and left the house. She jumped in the car to drive the two miles into the village. The roads were covered in a film of water from the rain, which hit the windscreen with full gusto as Lizzy increased the windscreen wipers to their fastest setting. By the time she'd pulled into an empty parking space outside the coffee shop, locked the car and run through the shop door, the rain had calmed to a slight drizzle, the type that leaves you feeling damp and uncomfortable.

"Morning, Lizzy!" Claire said as Lizzy walked through the door and hung her dripping coat on the coat rack beside the radiator in the hope it would dry out.

"Hi Claire. Do you want help with setting everything up this morning, or do you want me to get started on the cookies for the performance tomorrow?"

"If you can get started on the cookies, that would be great, thanks. Ooh, that's a nice bracelet. How long have you had that?" Claire nodded to Lizzy's wrist.

"My Secret Santa left me a gift of an advent calendar on my porch last night. Inside yesterday's door was this bracelet and the heart charm. Today's door had this yellow rose behind it. It means friendship, apparently." Lizzy smiled, twisting her wrist to allow the light to catch the charms. "The charms are meant to be extra clues to who my Secret Santa is, but so far, they tell me nothing I didn't already know."

"Well, don't worry too much. There are still five more days until Christmas, so hopefully the clues will become more revealing the nearer we get to Christmas

Eve." Claire patted Lizzy on the shoulder as she crossed behind the counter.

"I hope you're right." Lizzy sighed as she followed Claire into the kitchen to begin the marathon cookie bake for the ballet.

***

Lizzy finished decorating the last batch of cookies and peered up at the clock on the kitchen wall. It was three p.m. She had arranged to meet Peter at the Christmas tree farm at four, which meant she had exactly one hour to clean up the decorating and baking equipment, attempt to make herself look presentable—rather than covered head to toe in flour, icing sugar and edible glitter—and meet Peter.

The Christmas tree farm was situated a few miles out of the village and was run by the Sawyer family, who had lived and farmed in the area for generations. Lizzy pulled into the car park and walked towards the entrance. The whole front paddock had been decorated like a winter wonderland. Christmas trees adorned with twinkling fairy lights surrounded a little festive village scene with stalls selling decorations, hot chocolate, gifts and confectionery. Christmas music filled the air, and the atmosphere just screamed "Christmas". It was while she was strolling around the stalls that Lizzy spotted Peter over by the decorations stall, examining a set of hand-crafted glass baubles.

"Hi, Peter. Thanks for meeting me here." Lizzy gave him a side hug. "Wow, those baubles are amazing. The way the fairy lights catch the colours and glitter within the glass, it looks so magical!"

"Do you need any more decorations for your tree? Or do you have enough?" Peter asked.

"I have plenty, but I don't think I'll be able to pass up buying a set of those baubles!"

Turning to the stall holder, Lizzy made her purchase and accepted the bag of baubles.

"Okay, let's go and find the perfect tree!" Lizzy beamed at Peter. "Can we chop one down ourselves rather than pick a ready cut tree?"

Rolling his eyes, Peter walked into the farm office with her and took an axe from the counter assistant. They strode out into the field of Christmas trees ready to be felled.

Walking among the rows of fir, pine and spruce trees, Lizzy gazed at the different shapes, sizes and colours of the foliage.

"Which one takes your fancy?" Peter asked.

"Nothing yet. I don't want anything too big — it's going in the corner of the living room by the fireplace — so probably something like this." Lizzy pointed to a full-bodied, six-foot fir tree.

Preparing to strike the tree, Peter stood in a braced stance next to it and swung the axe.

"Peter, stop!" Lizzy called. "Can I do it please?"

Halting mid-swing, Peter glanced over to her. "Yeah, if you want to. Have you ever wielded an axe before though? Do you know how to do it?"

"No. Can you show me, please?"

Lizzy walked over to the tree. Peter took her by the shoulders and manoeuvred her into a suitable position. He handed her the axe, stood behind her and took her hands in his.

"Okay, so you need to stand with your legs slightly apart."

Lizzy followed Peter's directions.

"That's right. Now grip the axe and swing it back. Good, now we swing forward and hit the tree at a forty-five-degree angle."

Peter, still gripping the axe and Lizzy's hands, swung to hit the tree. The axe head cut into the wood. Peter helped Lizzy to free it from the trunk and take the next swing.

Five minutes later, they were smiling, satisfied, at the felled tree. Taking an end each, they picked it up and carried it to the cashier's booth to pay and return the axe.

"Hi Lizzy, hi Peter!" greeted Tess Sawyer, the owner of the farm. "That's a beauty of a tree you've found there. Do you need any help getting it out to your vehicle? Rick is around here somewhere; I can call him to give you a hand?"

"Hi Tess," Peter replied. "Thanks, but I think we should be able to manage it between the two of us. What do we owe you?"

"That's thirty pounds, please." Tess smiled politely.

Lizzy handed over the money and thanked her.

"Oh Lizzy, I have something for you!" Tess exclaimed as Lizzy turned to help Peter lift the tree again.

"For me?" Lizzy walked back to the counter and took the envelope Tess handed her.

"A very good-looking Santa dropped that off earlier and asked me to give it to you when you came in for your tree."

A little stunned, Lizzy realised this was her opportunity to get more information. "Do you mean you know who Santa is?"

"Yes, and I have been sworn to secrecy, so don't try to wheedle it out of me!" Tess laughed as Lizzy's face fell. "I will tell you one thing though." She leaned her elbows on the counter and her chin in her palms. "The whole village has thought you two were a match made in heaven from the moment you met. Everyone was surprised when nothing ever came of it. Although now it seems Santa has finally gathered the courage to declare his feelings. I just hope that you're gentle with him; he's a lovely lad, a real catch! You'd be mad not to love him back!"

"Thanks, Tess. I understand you've made a promise to Santa—I promise I won't put you on the spot. Well, Merry Christmas to you, Rick and the rest of the Sawyer family!"

Lizzy shoved the envelope in her coat pocket and leant down to lift her end of the Christmas tree on Peter's count.

***

"Thanks for helping with the tree today, it looks great." Standing back to admire the tree in its position beside the fireplace, Lizzy made a suggestion to Peter. "Do you want to stay and help decorate it? We can order in a pizza, put on some Christmas music and perhaps watch a Christmas movie afterwards?"

"Do you really think I don't know the real reason you want me to stay and help decorate the tree? It has nothing to do with that big box of tangled fairy lights over there, does it?" Peter chuckled, pointing over towards the aforementioned box.

Attempting to maintain a mock insulted expression, Lizzy looked at Peter with the puppy dog eyes she knew he could never resist.

"Oh, okay then, as long as we can get pepperoni pizza."

Peter gave in and sat down on the floor in front of the box of tangled lights, knowing it was pointless to argue. Looking at the mess in front of him, it was going to be a long evening.

***

Two hours and a large pepperoni pizza later, Lizzy and Peter sank down on the sofa to admire their handiwork. The house had been transformed into the centre-page spread of a Christmas interior design magazine. Garlands were draped on the mantelpiece and the banisters, bunches of mistletoe hung from every doorway, and the wreath of holly, pinecones and red ribbons on the front door bid a warm welcome to all visitors.

Lizzy flicked through the movie channels until she found a Christmas film they could watch. Peter went to the kitchen and returned with a huge bowl of popcorn and two mugs of steaming hot chocolate. Handing a mug to Lizzy, he grabbed the blanket from the back of the sofa and threw it over the two of them.

After a few minutes, Lizzy jumped up, startling him.

"Where are you going? The film is about to start!"

Lizzy rushed over to her coat hanging on the rack and fished around in the pockets to pull out a crumpled envelope.

"I forgot to open the letter from Santa that Tess gave me earlier," she explained as she tried in vain to flatten it out.

Rolling his eyes skywards and tutting, Peter pressed pause on the television remote and motioned for Lizzy to open the letter and read it.

She resumed her position next to Peter under the blanket and proceeded to open the envelope. Looking at the mystical writing on the parchment, Lizzy read it aloud to Peter.

My dearest Lizzy,

Thank you! You have helped me through some tough moments in my life, from the death of a beloved pet to my favourite teams being beat in the finals. You have teased me, joked with me and outright laughed at me, but I have always known that you care, just by the look in your eyes when you smile at me.

Next set of fun facts:

1. *I have stashed in a drawer at home three manuscripts which have taken me nearly 15 years to write but that I am too scared to send to a publisher. (I should definitely look into my fear of rejection!)*

2. *I was a volunteer whilst at college. I hated being alone in my dorm room, so went to chat to the residents of the local care home in the evenings, played games and read to them. It helped stem my loneliness.*

The next clue will be where there is grace and elegance, but you may have to go searching for it on tiptoes.

All my love,
Santa x

"Oh my gosh, this guy is spilling his deepest secrets!" Lizzy exclaimed.

"So, what do you think of it all then? Are you seriously considering this guy?" Peter asked.

"He seems genuine, and I must be close to him, based on what he says. I really think it is one of two people, both of whom I would be quite happy with seeing where the journey could take us if we decide to make a go of things," Lizzy shyly admitted.

"So, who's on your shortlist then?" Peter glanced at her, trying to entice information out of Lizzy without her clamming up completely.

"Promise you won't laugh or freak out?"

Turning to face Lizzy, Peter said, "Liz, I would never laugh when I know how important this is to you. You know you can tell me anything and I won't ever judge you."

"Thanks, Pete. I can't believe how lucky I am to have you as my best friend." Lizzy nervously picked at a frayed edge of the blanket. "I really feel a connection to Santa. If it's at all possible, I think I'm falling in love with him just through the letters and gifts. I know it's just a guess, but I really think it could be either Mark or James," she admitted, not able to look Peter in the eye.

"Mark as in my brother, and James as in the jerk that ripped your heart out?" Peter scoffed, a little shocked.

"Yes!" Lizzy cried with her head in her hands. "I know James broke my heart all those years ago, but he really is a nice guy, and I've always liked Mark."

"What? Really? How did I miss that one?" Peter exclaimed with disbelief.

"Every girl in school had a crush on Mark!"

"Yeah, don't I know it. Do you know how difficult it was living with him and his massive ego? I just didn't realise that you liked him too," Peter said, looking slightly stunned and uncharacteristically reserved.

Smirking at Peter's obvious jealousy, Lizzy decided to tease him some more. "What's wrong with all the girls liking Mark? Unless, of course, you were jealous of all the attention he got? Oh, was there someone you had a crush on that liked Mark instead of you?"

"What?! Umm, no, don't be silly. No, it was just mad living with him rubbing it in my face the whole time," Peter rambled, unable to keep eye contact with Lizzy.

"Right, okay then, if you say so," Lizzy giggled, winking at Peter.

Rolling his eyes, Peter knew when he was beaten and decided to make a hasty exit before Lizzy could probe any deeper into his teenage love life.

"Well, I better be heading off. I have to help Mrs Shaw, the drama teacher, with the set for the ballet tomorrow. Are you going to watch it?" he asked as he put his jacket on and picked up his keys.

"What! I thought we were going to watch a Christmas film?"

"Yeah, sorry, it's getting quite late and I don't want to be tired in the morning — it's going to be a long day!" Peter blurted as an explanation.

"Oh, okay then, not to worry. We can watch the film any time," Lizzy replied. "Umm, I was planning on watching the ballet; I haven't seen *The Nutcracker* for years. It should be fun."

"Well, I'll see you tomorrow night then. Thanks for the pizza," Peter called over his shoulder as he walked out the front door and down the path to his truck parked on the road, leaving Lizzy staring after him.

CHAPTER NINE

When Lizzy woke the next morning it was to a blanket of white outside. Overnight, there had been another snowfall, which brought a crisp chill to the winter air and decorated the trees and roofs with glistening icicles and swirling frost patterns. After closing the bedroom curtains against the freezing world outside, Lizzy made her way downstairs to the kitchen and turned on the kettle.

Eagerly, she reached for the advent calendar and opened the door engraved with the ornate number twenty. Peering inside, she pulled out another note and a small felt drawstring gift bag. Inside the bag was another charm for her bracelet, this time in the shape of a hockey stick.

Confusion etched on her face, Lizzy unfolded the note and began to read.

My dearest Lizzy,

As you already know, I am mad about ice hockey. It was always a dream of mine to be an NHL hockey player, but alas, my skating or hockey skills have never reached the required standard.

I promise that my letters will be more revealing from now on. I think I am still frightened that you'll realise who I am and turn me down. I don't want to ruin our friendship; you mean the world to me.

With all my love,
Santa x

With the charm added to her bracelet, Lizzy prepared her cup of tea and leaned against the sink, gazing out of the kitchen window. She sipped the tea and let the liquid warm her from the inside out.

Pondering the charm and the note, Lizzy came to the conclusion that she was no nearer to learning Santa's identity than she was yesterday. Her three prime suspects were still Mark, James and Peter, and the latest clue could link to any one of them.

After getting dressed, she headed out to the car, stomping her way through the thin layer of snow which had settled on the ground. She turned the key in the engine and whacked the heat on full blast before gingerly edging out onto the road and making her way into the village. She parked in front of the coffee shop and entered.

The shop was cosy. A fire was burning in the grate, creating a warm glow that reached all four corners of the room. There were already a few customers scattered around the room, drinking tea, coffee and hot chocolate and eating the gorgeous treats Claire and Lizzy had baked the day before.

Lizzy hung up her coat and made her way through the tables to the kitchen. That was when she saw the denim-clad legs sticking out from the bottom of the oven.

"Erm, hello?" Lizzy asked hesitantly.

The legs moved, and from underneath the oven, the rest of the body appeared.

"Hey Lizzy, how are you?" James smiled.

A little shocked at seeing her ex at her place of work, Lizzy asked, "What are you doing here?"

Just at that moment, Claire bustled in from the front of the shop carrying a tray of dirty crockery and cutlery ready for the dishwasher.

"Oh, Lizzy, hi—I didn't realise you were here already. Thank you for coming in on your day off! I called James in to take a look at the oven as the door was getting stuck again."

Sending a polite smile in James's direction, Lizzy hurried around the kitchen, a little flustered. Since their break-up, she'd been polite enough to make small talk whenever she bumped into James, but it had always been slightly awkward.

"Lizzy, can you make a start on the order for the refreshment stand for the ballet performance tonight, please? I think the order slip is on the noticeboard." Claire directed Lizzy to the board, where she had pinned up the order from Mrs Shaw.

"Wow, this order is huge!" Lizzy looked at Claire in disbelief. "She really wants all of this for one refreshment stand?"

"Yep, she has the whole of the dance school plus their families attending, not to mention most of the village. I'll be able to help you later on, but for now, I'll cover the shop if you can negotiate with James here about getting the oven in good working order so we can bake that long list." Claire winked at Lizzy as she hurried back out into the front of the shop.

Feeling a little out of place in their own kitchen, Lizzy began busying herself preparing the different bowls of batter for the various cakes and biscuits. An hour later, she had reached the stage where she could go no further without the use of the oven. Lizzy broached the subject with James, who was still waist deep under the oven.

"Erm, James, how long will it be until I can use the oven?"

"Give me five more minutes. I'm just fixing the last screws back in place then I should be done."

When he raised his head once again, it was to a flustered-looking Lizzy surrounded by baking trays full of cake mix and biscuit batter, all waiting for the oven.

"Wow, you've been busy!" James exclaimed, open mouthed. "I didn't know you could work so fast!"

"Well, the order is massive and I need to make sure everything cools in time for us to decorate them."

"Do you have a date for the show tonight?" James asked, glancing up at Lizzy from the floor, but unable to meet her eyes.

"No, I was just going to go on my own. I need to help Claire lay out the refreshment stall, but apart from that I'm free," Lizzy explained pretending that the pan of batter in front of her needed her full attention in order to avoid looking at James.

She didn't know if he was just making conversation or if he was actually asking her out. She also didn't know how she felt about it. Was James Santa? She wasn't so sure. If he was asking her out, why would he bother continuing to send the letters?

"Well, would you like to come along with me? We haven't really had a chance to talk since we broke up, and I miss you." James still couldn't look Lizzy in the eye.

Intrigued, Lizzy accepted his invitation. "That will be nice; it will be a chance to catch up. Shall I meet you there, say at seven thirty?" she smiled.

"Perfect, I'm looking forward to it already." James grinned as he gathered up his tools and picked up the toolbox.

He gave Lizzy a peck on the cheek, exited the kitchen, said farewell to Claire and left the shop.

"Well, how did it go?" Claire eagerly hissed as she stuck her head round the kitchen door.

"We're meeting at the show tonight, and hopefully we can clear the air. Now, let me get on with this order, otherwise nothing will be ready for tonight!" Lizzy laughed as she shooed Claire from the kitchen.

***

In the theatre foyer prior to the performance, Lizzy and Claire began setting up the refreshment table in time for the audience's arrival.

"Ooh, I was wondering when you two would turn up. I'm starving!" Peter exclaimed as he seemed to appear out of nowhere and began to rummage through the boxes of treats.

Slapping his hand, Claire laughed. "Oi! You get your mitts out of those boxes. You'll have to wait until we've set up, like everyone else!"

Sneakily grabbing a cookie from a box, Peter threw a cheeky wink at Lizzy before biting into the cookie and receiving a clout on the arm from an annoyed Claire.

"Ow, there's no need for violence!" Peter ducked behind Lizzy and held her out as a barrier between himself and Claire.

"Hey, don't use me as your human shield!" Lizzy giggled, trying to escape from his grip.

"But you're so good at it! And she's scary!" Peter nodded his head towards Claire, who was shaking her head in annoyance as she continued to unpack the baked goods onto the display table.

The next thing they knew, the front doors were opened and hordes of people buzzing with excitement entered the foyer. Looking up, Claire spotted James making his way towards them.

"Oh, Lizzy, your date is on his way over!"

"Date? What date?" Peter's brow creased with confusion and intrigue as Lizzy glared at Claire.

Ignoring Lizzy, Claire explained to Peter, "James was kind enough to fix the oven at the coffee shop this morning, and it seems that during their time in the kitchen together, he asked Lizzy out. He apparently wants to catch up and clear the air after their break up."

"What? You cannot be serious!" Peter looked incredulously at Lizzy as a determined look appeared on her face. "You haven't agreed to talk with him? After what he put you through? Liz, please think about this."

"Peter, I am perfectly capable of running my own life. I don't need you or Claire telling me how to live it. We're just meeting to have a chat; it's not like I've accepted a marriage proposal!"

Taking her in a sideways hug, Peter sighed. "I realise that, but we don't want him to hurt you like the last time. We both love you and care too much to allow him to crush you again."

Squeezing Peter's waist, Lizzy attempted to reassure him. "I know you're worried about me, but don't worry, I won't let him hurt me again."

With that, James reached the table and greeted them all. "Hi Lizzy, Claire, Peter—how are you all?" Not waiting for a reply, he continued, "So, Lizzy, shall we take our seats? I think the show is about to start."

Glancing up, Lizzy gave Peter a reassuring smile, which he reciprocated, before threading her arm through James's as he led her into the theatre.

The conversation was stilted at first. They took their seats and chatted about the upcoming performance.

"Wow, Peter has done an amazing job on those backdrops!" Lizzy commented, taking in the beautiful winter wonderland scene and the wooden trees in the foreground.

"Yeah, I suppose it's okay for an am-dram performance." James shot the snide remark.

It came as no surprise to Lizzy. James and Peter had always had a heated relationship, which went downhill drastically when Lizzy and James broke up. Lizzy was glad that James had stayed away after college, as she feared that if Peter had come in contact with him, he may have ended up admitted to the local hospital.

Ignoring the comment, Lizzy decided to change tack. "So, what have you been up to since college?"

"I got a position at a marketing firm in Boston, stayed there for ten years and worked my way up through the ranks. I'm now running my own firm with thirty staff beneath me. Do you know, I haven't really missed home that much at all? Of course, I visited my parents for Christmas and Easter, but Boston is a great city and there was nothing drawing me back here."

Feeling a little put out that James didn't think his family, friends and herself were worth coming home for, Lizzy probed a little further. "What about hobbies? What do you do in your spare time?"

"Oh, I don't have any spare time really — starting my own firm has seen to that. Not that I mind. The most important thing to me at the moment is to succeed and to make my firm the top one in Boston."

"So, you don't do anything to unwind? Like play sports, visit art galleries, write, socialise, et cetera?"

Lizzy quizzed, with a growing suspicion that she was not sitting next to Santa.

"Heavens no!" James exclaimed, almost horrified. "Writing stories and looking at art is such a waste of time. The only time I play sports is when I meet a client for a game of golf."

The lights dimmed, and onto the stage walked Mrs Shaw to introduce the performance. Lizzy was silently thankful for the interruption; this definitely wasn't the James she'd been in love with during her teens. He had changed a lot, and not for the better. She couldn't wait for tonight to be over.

The children pranced around the stage to the music, the concentration showing on their faces. Lizzy recognised most of them from the coffee shop, but there was one little girl who danced with such feeling that Lizzy could almost feel herself being taken back to her own childhood when she used to don her tutu and dance around the trees in the local woods, pretending to be the sugarplum fairy. She had dreamed of being a famous ballet dancer and performing in the New York Ballet, but her parents had said she needed to concentrate on her failing schoolwork and pulled her out of dance classes to improve her grades.

She knew there were adult ballet classes at the community centre, and if she could find the courage, she would love to step back into her pointe shoes, but that was her biggest problem: she lacked courage and self-confidence. Lizzy had no clue as to why Santa, whoever he was, had these feelings for her. She couldn't understand how anyone could love and care for her that way. That kind of magic only happened in fairy tales and movies.

Lizzy was so engrossed in her thoughts that she didn't realise the first half was over until the house lights came back on and the curtain dropped on the stage.

Turning in his chair to face her, James not-so-casually swung an arm round Lizzy's shoulders and curled his lip up in the smirk that she used to adore, but now just made her cringe.

Gazing at Lizzy, James made a suggestion. "So how about we skip the second half and go for a drink at the pub instead? Ballet really is dull, don't you agree?"

Lizzy could feel her blood begin to boil and her skin crawl. Had James always been this rude? The children were trying their best, and she was enjoying their performance. He really didn't know her at all, if he thought she hated the ballet and would want to leave halfway through.

"Oh, I can't, I'm afraid. I promised Claire I would help her with the refreshment stand during the interval and at the end. In fact, I'd better head out there now before she sends a search party to find me. It's been nice catching up with you, James, have a great Christmas and please send my best wishes to your family." Lizzy couldn't get out of the theatre and into the foyer fast enough.

Catching the look on her friend's face, Claire asked, "I take it the date didn't go as planned then?"

"Oh my god, no! He's changed so much since school. He's so smarmy and rude."

"Really? Boston has obviously had a negative effect on him then. It looks like you had a lucky escape," Claire said, visibly shocked.

"I just hope he isn't Santa! Can you imagine how awkward that will be?"

"Oh, speaking of Santa, he dropped this off for you!" Claire smiled, handing Lizzy another envelope.

"What? He actually gave it to you in person? So you know who he is?" Lizzy gasped.

"Yes, I do, and I've also been sworn to secrecy, which as you know is not easy for me!"

"Can you at least put my mind at rest? Please tell me it isn't James."

Shaking her head, Claire smiled at Lizzy with a mischievous glint in her eyes. "I have been sworn to secrecy, sorry."

Frowning at her friend, Lizzy opened the envelope and read out loud to Claire.

My dearest Lizzy,

I know your secret — you wanted to be a ballerina up until we went to secondary school. I once saw you practising your pirouettes in the woods when you thought no one was around. I don't know why you kept that talent a secret. You were magical, you performed flawlessly, and even though I couldn't hear the music you were listening to through your headphones, I could imagine it due to the story your body told through the flow and movement. You showed me a more gentle, majestic side to you, which I always knew was hidden inside, but you looked so happy and at peace when you danced. I could watch you for hours.

I will admit that the closer we get to Christmas Eve, the more nervous I am.

The next clue will reveal a whole lot s'more.

All my love,

Santa x

Lizzy looked at Claire a little sheepishly, knowing that she had never admitted her secret talent.

"Wow, I never knew you loved to dance! Why didn't you take lessons?" Claire asked.

"I did when I was little, but my schoolwork suffered so my parents took me out of the classes so I could concentrate on school," Lizzy explained.

"Well, you should definitely add it to your New Year's resolutions for next year!"

"I don't know about that, but there is one thing I am sure of—and slightly relieved about—and that's that this letter proves James isn't Santa. From the conversation we just had, he didn't know about my love of ballet."

Claire just smiled at Lizzy and gave her a wink in confirmation.

"Oh, this is so frustrating, I just want it to be Christmas Eve already. Although, I have narrowed it down to two candidates: the Henley brothers. It must be Mark!" Lizzy exclaimed, grinning from ear to ear.

Seeing where this line of conversation was dangerously heading, Claire cut in. "As I said earlier…"

"Yes, I know, you cannot confirm or deny who it is," Lizzy jumped in, the frustration oozing from her voice.

The rest of the evening passed without incident. The children performed wonderfully through the second half, and once the performance was over, the whole cast and crew ascended the stage to take a bow. It was then that Lizzy spotted something that set the cogs in her brain turning. There, standing at the back, was Peter, looking quite green around the gills, and Mark standing next to him. So Mark had been present—he could definitely be Santa!

Manning the refreshment stand after the performance, Lizzy and Claire were greeted by Mark and a very pasty-looking Peter.

"Hey, you two. Have you got any ginger ale left for Peter?" Mark asked with a smirk.

Edging round the table, Lizzy looked up at Peter's face and put her palm to his forehead.

"You really don't look great, Peter. What's wrong?"

"It's nothing, I'll be fine in a minute. Mark loves taking the mick out of me for my fear of heights," Peter mumbled, wishing the attention would be pulled away from him. "I've just spent the last two hours up on the gantry, manoeuvring the scenery."

"Well, why don't you go outside and grab some fresh air?" Claire suggested.

With that, Peter gave a half-hearted wave and made his way through the throng of people to the exit and the cool, crisp night air.

"I'd better go and check he's okay," Mark announced, his gaze following Peter as he exited the building. "I'm not a fan of heights myself, but I didn't realise how bad he still got with it." He put his hat and scarf on over his thick winter jacket. "Hey, are you both going to the Christmas campfire tomorrow night?"

Claire jumped in to answer before Lizzy could even formulate a response in her mind. "Yes, we'll be there. Will we see you?"

"If you're going to be there then I definitely will be," Mark exclaimed, throwing a broad smile at the two girls before he turned to follow Peter outside. "See you tomorrow!"

Grinning at a bemused Lizzy, Claire began whistling the tune to "Santa Claus is Coming to Town" as she cleaned up the refreshment stand.

"Oh, shut up!" Lizzy laughed, with a red flush to her face as she busied herself to hide her embarrassment.

CHAPTER TEN

It was early evening and the whole village had turned out to enjoy the Christmas campfire in a large clearing in the woods. In the centre of the clearing was a large fire with logs positioned around it. The village folk were gathered in small groups, talking and enjoying the Christmas spirit, not to mention the toasting of marshmallows and eating of s'mores.

Lizzy was serving hot chocolate and mince pies from a stand near the entrance of the clearing. Mark and Peter strolled over and placed their order for two hot chocolates.

"Lizzy, Peter tells me you don't get out much socially," Mark said. "Would you like to come skating the day after tomorrow, just like we used to?"

Raising an eyebrow in surprise, Lizzy glanced at Peter. She could tell he was uncomfortable with the conversation, probably because he realised his brother had just successfully landed him in trouble with her.

Smiling politely, Lizzy responded, "Thanks, Mark, that would be great. Shall I meet you at the rink around two p.m.?"

"Perfect. Bring Claire if you like, and I'll drag this one with me." Mark nudged Peter with his elbow as Peter threw him an annoyed glare. "It could be just like the old days!" Mark beamed at Lizzy.

"Oh, okay, thanks," Lizzy said, with a look of confusion etched on her face. "I'll go and see if she's available."

Placing a sign on the table telling the patrons to "Help yourself", Lizzy made her way across the clearing to where Claire was chatting to a group of elderly ladies, regulars from the coffee shop. Lizzy waited patiently for Claire to finish her conversation before catching her attention.

"Hey Lizzy, are you having a good time?" Claire asked, picking up on the puzzled look on Lizzy's face.

"I have just had the oddest conversation with Mark. He asked me out to the ice-skating rink but then turned it into an all-friends-welcome gathering. I don't know what to make of it."

"What do you mean, Mark asked you out but turned it into a friendly gathering?" Claire asked wrinkling up her nose.

"I thought he was asking me out because he's the Secret Santa," Lizzy admitted shyly.

"What? Do you want it to be Mark?"

"Yes, I think so. You know I had a crush on him throughout school, but he didn't seem to notice me then. When he invited me, I put two and two together. However, now I'm not too sure, because he told me to bring a friend."

"Well, don't worry. If he is Santa, you'll find out soon enough. Just go to the skating rink and enjoy yourself. I'll come with you as your friend to keep you out of mischief." Claire smirked.

"Okay, I guess you're right. I can't believe how quickly Christmas has caught up with us; it's been non-stop the past couple of weeks," Lizzy mused.

"I reckon that has a lot to do with your mind being preoccupied on finding out who the mysterious Santa is. You've had to attend all the social functions because the clues were hidden there."

"I never realised, but you're right—Santa has had me out and about much more than I usually would be. I normally avoid all the Christmas hubbub and stay indoors during the evenings," Lizzy said as the realisation dawned. Santa knew she was a bit of a hermit when it came to going out and socialising, so he'd forced her hand to get her out of her cocoon.

"Well, I don't know about you, but I'm going to get myself a s'more. Are you coming?" Claire asked as they were joined by Mark and Peter.

"Definitely. S'mores are the best thing ever!" Lizzy grinned, taking hold of Claire's elbow as they made their way over to the campfire.

She sat down between Claire and Peter, turning to her best friend.

"Hey, Pete. Are you okay after last night? You looked rough."

"Yeah, I'm fine, thanks. It was nothing, just felt a little giddy after being up on the gantry all evening, peering down onto the stage." Peter smiled, a little embarrassed.

Mark chose this moment to lean around in front of Claire to quiz Lizzy on Santa. "Hey Lizzy, Claire's been filling me in on your dramatic Christmas treasure hunt. Have you found today's clue yet?"

A little startled by his openness on the subject, Lizzy responded, "I haven't found the letter yet, but today's door of the advent calendar contained another note and a dog charm for this gorgeous bracelet."

Lizzy held out her wrist to show them the charm bracelet as she remembered the note she'd found in the advent calendar:

My dearest Lizzy,
I can always remember when you comforted me after we lost Sooky. You got me through that difficult time, and I am forever thankful.
With all my love,
Santa x

"I don't get it," Claire exclaimed. "What's a dog got to do with Christmas?"

"It's a clue to the identity of Santa. Sometime in our friendship, a dog has meant something to the both of us," Lizzy explained.

The note had said as much. What Lizzy didn't disclose was that she was now certain Santa was one of the Henley brothers. Sooky was the gorgeous golden retriever the Henleys had throughout their early childhood. When she had passed over the rainbow bridge during the boys' teenage years, Lizzy had comforted both Mark and Peter in their grief.

Throwing glances at both the brothers, Lizzy couldn't see any changes in either of their facial expressions. They both would be masters at poker; neither so much as flinched or smirked knowingly when she mentioned the clue.

"Oh. Well, what do you think then?" Claire pushed for answers. "Could it still be who you mentioned yesterday?"

Not believing that Claire was trying to get her to name her suspects in front of Mark and Peter, Lizzy tried to turn the subject to the s'mores they were toasting.

"I really don't know. We'll have to see who it is on Christmas Eve." She looked at Mark, who had marshmallow and melted chocolate dribbling down his chin. "You are making an absolute mess of that s'more; how on earth did you manage that?"

Grinning broadly, Mark shrugged. "I have no idea. Perhaps you better show me how it should be done."

Lizzy turned to the table containing the ingredients and skewers for toasting the marshmallows and gathered up the items she needed. It was then that she noticed the envelope and remembered the clue from the previous day: *The next clue will reveal a whole lot s'more.*

Envelope in hand, Lizzy turned back to the group and showed them the letter. Feeling a little embarrassed to read it out loud in front of who she thought was the author, Lizzy made the excuse that it was too dark to read it properly, so she put it in her pocket and continued to prepare the s'more for Mark.

"So how do you feel about this mystery man declaring his undying love for you in letters?" Mark asked Lizzy with a glint in his eye.

Still feeling slightly self-conscious, but knowing that she shouldn't give any hint that she knew he was Santa, Lizzy answered Mark's question honestly.

"It was bizarre at first. I wasn't sure I believed it, but as the letters continued, I started looking forward to them. I realised that the author was genuine and had a deep connection with me. It may sound odd, but I think I have fallen in love with him through the letters even though I don't know who he is yet."

All three friends were staring at Lizzy, awestruck. It was Claire who spoke first.

"Lizzy, seriously, how can you fall in love with a piece of paper?"

"It's hard to explain, but he gets me. It feels like we are connected and are meant to be together, like soulmates."

Mark was smiling as Lizzy fumbled with her explanation. Claire looked like a child on Christmas morning, seeing the presents under the tree for the first time.

Lizzy shyly looked towards Peter for support but was greeted by stunned silence, his mouth opening and closing as he tried to formulate words. All of a sudden, he got up from the log they were perched on, mumbling something about needing to get a drink, and walked over to the drinks table on the other side of the clearing. Watching Peter escape the group, Mark made his excuses and followed him.

Lizzy watched from afar the conversation between the brothers. Illuminated by a couple of hurricane lamps standing either end of the drinks table, it was obvious that Mark and Peter were having an animated conversation. Mark was frequently looking over at Lizzy and Claire, while Peter kept his back to them the whole time. After a while, the pair returned, all evidence of the conversation gone, but Lizzy could tell by the way Peter couldn't maintain eye contact with her that he was angry at something she had said or done.

The rest of the evening passed by with more s'mores and marshmallows being enjoyed. Gazing into the flames of the fire as they licked the charred logs, Lizzy didn't realise her name was being called until a hand tapped her on the shoulder, bringing her out of her reverie.

"Hey Lizzy, is anyone sitting here?" Mark motioned to the empty space on the log beside her.

"No, Mark, please take a seat. Sorry, I was miles away—flames always have a knack of taking me off into a dream world. They're so mesmerising."

Mark just chuckled. "Don't worry about it. I remember how you and Peter used to stare into the flames and point out the different shapes in the shadows, making up stories and creating characters. If I remember rightly, they always had pun names like Ashley Ashton, Fiona Flame and Charlie Charcoal."

"Gosh, yes, I remember that now." Lizzy laughed. "We used to wind you and Claire up something terrible with the completely random stories which were totally unrealistic."

"Ah ha! There's that gorgeous laugh I've missed all this time. Are you okay, Lizzy?" Mark asked, concern etched on his features. "You don't seem your usual happy self recently."

"I'm fine. I just think that the Santa letters have highlighted to me how lonely I was, and I didn't know it. I hope that Santa is really genuine, and I can love him like he loves me." Lizzy sighed and stared into the flames once more. "I suppose I'm scared that I will hurt his feelings if I don't feel the same way about him. He's cared for me his whole life, and I don't want to be the person that brings his world crashing down and stomps on his hopes and dreams. I'd be devastated if that were to happen to me."

Nodding in understanding, Mark put his arm comfortingly around her shoulders and pulled her into a side hug. "It will all be fine, you'll see. I have a strong feeling that when you find out the identity of Santa, everything will fall into place and you won't need to worry about feeling lonely anymore."

"I hope you're right," Lizzy said, then stood and straightened out her coat, hat and gloves. "I better be off home soon—I need to be up early tomorrow. I volunteered to help set up the theatre for the Christmas film night. Are you and Peter going to pop along and watch some?"

"Yeah, that sounds like fun. I'll drag Mr Grumpy with me too—hopefully a Christmas film will cheer him up," Mark said as he motioned with his thumb over his shoulder in Peter's direction. "I don't know what's wrong with him this year; he's usually full of the Christmas spirit."

Smiling at Mark, Lizzy bid him farewell and raised her hand in a goodbye wave to Claire and Peter, who were talking to Bob, the postman, across the fire pit.

***

By the time Lizzy got home, the temperature had dropped to well below freezing. The weather forecast had suggested a cold front was coming in from the north bringing heavy snowfall within the next day or two. Lizzy carefully stoked the fire, made herself a large mug of hot chocolate and sat down on the sofa to read the next letter from Santa.

Opening the envelope, she could smell the scent of fresh pine. She had never noticed this on the other letters. Everything else about the letter was the same as the previous ones, even down to the wax seal.

My dearest Lizzy,

I so wish I could say that to your face. I know you are anxious about meeting me and finding out my identity, but I just want to let you know that I do not want you to feel pressured. If you do not feel the same way about me as I feel for you then we can forget the whole thing and I will try to move on with my life. It will take time, but I really don't want to jeopardise our lifelong friendship. It means too much to me. You mean too much to me!

So, you have probably narrowed your suspect list down to two or three by now. I honestly don't think I will be on the list at all, but I desperately wish I am.

The next clue will be in amongst the reels.

All my love,
Santa x

Feeling her heart skip a beat, Lizzy rose from the sofa, turned off the living room lights and walked up the stairs to bed, hopeful that when sleep came, it brought with it warm dreams of Santa.

CHAPTER ELEVEN

Lizzy stretched under the warm covers of her bed, sticking a foot out to test the temperature. She shuddered and quickly pulled it back into her cosy cocoon of blankets, sheets and pillows. Suddenly, a pillow landed on her head from the doorway. Groaning in annoyance, Lizzy gingerly stuck the top of her head out from the blanket and cracked open one eye against the bright light now streaming in through the open curtains.

"Come on, Lazy Lizzy! Shift it! We promised the vicar we would help set up the theatre for film night." Peter smirked as he reached under the blanket to tickle Lizzy's feet.

Shrieks filled the bedroom as Peter's cold hands met Lizzy's toasty feet. Kicking his hands away, Lizzy jumped out of the bed looking very rumpled and annoyed.

"Alright, alright, I'm up! You are pure evil, you know!" she hissed as she barged past Peter and headed for the bathroom.

Hearing his laughter behind her, she shut the door and turned on the shower to heat the water.

***

By the time Lizzy had finished dressing and drying her hair, Peter had prepared breakfast for the both of them and was sitting down at the kitchen counter reading the morning newspaper while eating his toast.

"There's fresh tea in the pot if you want some, and I cooked eggy bread for you too," he said as he nudged the plate of French toast towards Lizzy.

"This looks great, thanks, but what are you doing here so early?" she asked.

"I know you too well, Liz. I bet you got home last night, went pretty much straight up to bed and forgot to set an alarm to get you up on time." Peter explained with a knowing smirk on his lips.

Knowing he had her pegged, Lizzy mumbled, "Something like that, yeah."

Chuckling to himself, Peter leant over Lizzy and pinched a piece of her eggy bread. Slapping his hand was a futile effort as he popped the bread in his mouth and gave her a cheeky wink.

"Oh, I haven't opened my advent calendar yet!" Lizzy exclaimed as she jumped down from the stool and reached for the calendar.

Behind the door, she found another felt gift bag and a note.

"Whatcha get?" Peter asked through a mouth full of eggy bread.

Lizzy tipped the contents of the gift bag out into her hand; it was another charm for her bracelet. This time it was a padlock. A little confused, Lizzy unravelled the note, hoping for an explanation.

My dearest Lizzy,

You hold the key to my heart, just like you used to hold my locker key in secondary school because I was forever misplacing it.

I wouldn't have survived if it hadn't been for you telling me which lessons I had and when. I think forgetfulness definitely runs in my family; my brother is exactly the same.

All my love,

Santa x

"It's a beautiful padlock charm to add to my bracelet." Lizzy held the charm out for Peter to examine. She removed the bracelet from her wrist and attached the new charm.

"So do you have any further thoughts as to who Santa is?" Peter hesitantly asked.

"Yes, I think I know who it is, but I'd rather not say anything just yet in case I'm wrong. I don't want to get my hopes up or make a fool of myself," Lizzy gingerly explained, casting her eyes down as she fiddled with the bracelet.

"Hey!" Peter took her shoulders and gently raised her chin with his finger to make her look up at him. "You have nothing to worry about. We all have been embarrassed at some point in our lives. But remember this, Liz: you will always have me to fall back on if you need someone to cushion the blow and a shoulder to cry on."

Smiling a watery smile, Lizzy lifted her arms up to circle Peter's neck as she drew him into a hug.

"I know you've got my back, thank you! And don't forget that I'll always be here for you too!"

Reciprocating the hug, Peter wrapped his arms around Lizzy's waist and smiled into her hair as he rested his chin on the top of her head.

"Right, that's enough mushy talk for today," he announced. "Let's get to the theatre and help set up for tonight."

Grinning at his obvious discomfort, Lizzy grabbed her bag and put on her coat, hat and gloves and pushed Peter out the front door towards his truck, grabbing his keys from the kitchen counter as they went.

"Right, we better get a move on," she said.

"Yep, do you want me to drive you?" Peter offered. "I'll drop you home later on."

"You've got yourself a deal!" Lizzy grinned, throwing the truck keys to Peter.

***

The journey to the theatre was a quiet one. There was a slight unspoken tension between them that Lizzy felt needed to be addressed.

"You and Mark seemed very animated last night—was everything okay?"

"Yes, fine thanks. It was just a brotherly disagreement, but we sorted it out," Peter reassured her, all the while not taking his eyes off the road.

The more Lizzy thought about the situation, the more she felt he was lying to her. Something was definitely going on between the Henley brothers!

They pulled into the theatre car park, and Peter manoeuvred the truck into an available space.

Walking into the theatre they were greeted by Mr Simms, the vicar, looking rather flustered.

"Ah, Peter, excellent—we can use your mechanical prowess with the projector. I can't seem to get it working properly."

Peter didn't have the chance to take his coat off before Mr Simms had grabbed him by the arm and pulled him in the direction of the projector booth. Grinning at the sight of Peter being herded away, Lizzy turned to the rest of the group gathered in the foyer to get her instructions for the day.

***

It took all day, but the small group of six worked tirelessly to set up the theatre so that by the time the first members of the audience arrived to take their seats, the whole place had been transformed with Christmas trees and garlands adorned with twinkling lights and decorations. However, not everything was going to plan. Peter and Mr Simms were still struggling with the projector.

Heading up to the projector room to check on the progress, Lizzy bumped into Peter coming down the stairs.

"Hey, have you got the projector working yet? Some of the audience have already arrived and are settling into their seats."

"Hey, Liz. No, not yet—I've just got to run out to the truck and get a different screwdriver; this one is too small for the screw heads on the projector." Peter held up the screwdriver as he squeezed past Lizzy and jogged down the stairs.

Up the stairs, Lizzy entered the projector room to find Mr Simms with sleeves rolled up to his elbows, covered in grease from the projector.

"Hello, Lizzy, my dear. How is it all going downstairs? Peter seems to think he has finally worked out the issue, so we should be up and running in no time."

Lizzy looked around the room. Bits and pieces of the projector's mechanism lay scattered on every flat surface. With a look of disbelief, she remarked, "No offence, Vicar, but by the look of this room, I would say we'll be lucky to see the film by New Year!"

Glancing round the room to see what she meant, the vicar said, "Oh, don't worry about the mess. Peter is a dab hand at mechanics; he'll have this back together in a jiffy. In fact, here he is now!"

Lizzy turned towards the door as Peter marched through with his toolbox in hand.

The vicar had been right. Within a few minutes, Peter had reassembled the mechanism and had the projector running. From a nearby table covered in film reels, Peter selected the first one and set it up on the projector. It was then that Lizzy noticed an envelope sticking out from in between a stack of film reels on the table. Remembering the last clue, *The next clue will be in amongst the reels,* Lizzy went over to the table and carefully pulled the envelope out.

Noticing her movement, Peter smiled at her.

"Another gift from Santa?"

"Yes, it's the next clue," Lizzy explained, holding up the letter.

Opening the envelope, Lizzy was surprised to find not only an ornately written letter, just like all the rest, but also a remarkable sketch of herself sitting in the coffee shop, laughing at something she'd just been told. The artist had used pencil, and by the looks of it had either drawn it from a photograph or from life. The latter unnerved Lizzy somewhat, to think that she had been sitting, laughing and chatting freely with the customers while someone was watching her and drawing her. It was only when she read the letter that she realised the situation wasn't as creepy as she'd first thought.

My dearest Lizzy,

I drew the picture from a memory of you sitting in the coffee shop, laughing at a joke someone had told you. Your face visits me in my dreams every night, and I have this image of you etched in my memory. You are all I can think about; you distract me without even being in my presence.

I feel like a lovesick teenager around you. I get tongue-tied and lose myself in your staggering beauty so much that I just find myself staring at you at times, wishing that I could be with you all the time—to wake up to your face every morning and tell you I love you before closing my eyes at night, to be whisked away to a dream world in the arms of Morpheus, visualising your face laughing and smiling, keeping me sane until we both wake up again and the cycle repeats itself.

You will have another letter and an advent calendar door to open tomorrow with your final clues.

On Christmas Eve, there will be an extra special gift behind the advent door. Please open it first thing. I will be giving out presents at the children's hospital on Christmas Eve morning. Hopefully I will see you then.

The next clue will be in the cupboards in the ice palace.
All my love,
Santa x

Wiping the tears that tracked down her cheeks, Lizzy choked out, "Oh my gosh, if that's what he writes in a letter, can you imagine what his manuscripts are like? He has such a way with words!"

Taking Lizzy in his arms, Peter gently rubbed her back in a soothing motion. "He certainly can write a letter that hits the emotions, can't he?" he acknowledged.

Clearing her throat and pulling out of Peter's arms, Lizzy made her excuses and went back downstairs to the foyer to help the vicar greet the members of the audience and show them to their seats.

Sitting with Claire and Mark, Lizzy tried in vain to pay attention to the film on the screen, *The Muppet Christmas Carol*. Despite the roars of laughter from the audience and the giggling of the children in the front rows, Lizzy couldn't take her mind off the letter from Santa. The day after tomorrow was Christmas Eve; she would finally find out his true identity. All the clues had pointed towards Mark being Santa, and that fact was pleasing to Lizzy. Looking at him out of the corner of her eye, she checked out his profile — tall, with brown hair that always looked like it had half a tube of gel in it to keep it in place, clean shaven and those gorgeous blue eyes. Watching him carefully, she saw him turn a few times to make a joke with Claire. She had always loved his great sense of humour; he could make her laugh at the drop of a hat.

Allowing her mind to wander, Lizzy found herself dreaming of Christmas day, sitting on the sofa in Mark's arms in front of the roaring fire. Christmas tunes playing on the radio and the two of them sitting in a comfortable couple's silence, the type where neither party feels awkward, just perfectly suited to each other and satisfied to let the moment go by uninterrupted by speech.

It wasn't until Claire nudged her shoulder that Lizzy realised she had been staring at Mark. Luckily for her, his eyes were fixed on the film and hadn't noticed the attention. Claire on the other hand, took it as an opportunity to give Lizzy a pointed, exasperated look before smirking knowingly, shaking her head and turning back to watch the final scene.

The credits rolled across the screen and the house lights came back on. Murmuring voices grew louder as the audience slowly filed out of the theatre, through the foyer and into the cold winter night. Once everyone had departed, Lizzy and the band of organisers were left to clean up. Half an hour later, all litter had been picked up and put in bin bags, the tables in the foyer had been put away, and the film reels were boxed back up, ready to be returned to the hire company after Christmas and New Year.

Pulling on her coat, hat and gloves, Lizzy peered around, trying to spot Peter. She eventually caught sight of him coming down the stairs from the projector room.

"Hey, Liz. Are you ready to leave yet?" he asked. "Or do you need help with any more clearing up?"

After a quick glance round at the other members of the team putting on their own outdoor clothing, Lizzy smiled at Peter. "No, I think we're done. Shall we head off home?"

"Yeah, sure. I'll drop you back, unless I can persuade you that ordering takeaway is a great idea and we should stay up and watch some more Christmas films?" Peter gave her the biggest puppy dog eyes he could muster. Unfortunately for Lizzy, he knew that she couldn't resist his big blue eyes.

Rolling her eyes, Lizzy just giggled and nodded towards Peter's truck. "You are such a bad influence! What do you fancy? Chinese? Pizza? Indian?"

Grinning in victory, Peter opened the passenger door for Lizzy to get in and closed it behind her. Getting in the driver's side, Peter thought for a moment. "What about fish and chips? We haven't had that for ages!"

Nodding in agreement, Lizzy settled in the seat as Peter pulled out of the car park and headed in the direction of the fish and chip shop.

Chapter Twelve

It was the day before Christmas Eve, and the snow, which had been threatening with light flurries all week, had finally started to come down thick and fast.

Winter had always been Lizzy's favourite season. Most of her friends preferred the warmer seasons when they could spend the day at the beach, basking in the glorious summer sunshine whilst listening to the waves crashing on the shore, but Lizzy preferred the crisp, fresh air of the winter months, with the snow gently falling and covering everything in white. Wrapped up warm in hat, gloves, scarf, coat and boots, Lizzy went for a stroll along the fields and country lanes to clear her head and try to make sense of the Secret Santa letters and clues.

That morning, she had awoken and opened the door of the advent calendar to find another felt gift bag. When she'd tipped the contents into the palm of her hand, she'd smiled as she saw the yin-yang symbol on the charm. She'd opened the note attached, and read the words on the parchment.

My dearest Lizzy,

You are the yin to my yang; you complete me, and I do not know how I managed at college all those years without you beside me every day. I look forward to seeing you, and I feel empty if we do not meet up or speak each day.

Whenever I see you, my heart swells and I feel totally at peace. The thing I love the most about you is your laughter, from the little giggle to the infectious one that has you rolling around on the sofa or floor, crying and unable to catch your breath. The sound of your laugh is music to my ears; it turns my insides to mush, and I just want to hear it again and again.

All my love,

Santa x

Thinking of the letter, Lizzy walked in the cold air, enjoying the wind blowing the cobwebs away and allowing her to get a fresh perspective on what she wanted from life. Santa had opened her eyes to the possibility of finding her one true love, someone she could build a life with, marry and perhaps start a family, but most importantly, someone who would grow old with her and be her soulmate.

As she reached the lake just outside the village, Lizzy took in the view around her. Icicles hung from the trees. The lake itself was covered in a thick layer of ice, not quite ready for outdoor skating, but if the weather continued the way it had been then it would only take another day or two until children would be spinning around on skates, attempting triple axels or trying to score a goal with makeshift hockey pucks and sticks in a game of shinny.

Smiling to herself, Lizzy recalled skating hand in hand with Mark as he attempted, and succeeded, to pull a whiplash move that had her careering across the lake straight into a bush. She had recovered fairly quickly from the shock, but as Mark stood in front of her holding out a hand to help her up, she'd been more than happy to play the damsel in distress.

She realised, looking back, that their whole childhood had been peppered with little moments where Mark had shown his feelings towards her. She'd just always thought he—and Peter—had been looking out for her like they did each other, like she was the missing Henley sister.

Looking at the time on her phone, Lizzy noted that she was meant to be meeting Mark, Claire and Peter at the ice rink in two hours. That gave her enough time to walk back home, have a bite to eat and drive into the village.

***

The ice rink was situated just off the village square, where the friends had agreed to meet by the Christmas tree at two p.m. Lizzy was the first to arrive, which was a rarity as she was usually late for meet-ups.

She had only been there for a few minutes when she spotted Mark and Peter walking from the church car park. Claire could be seen exiting the coffee shop, where she had finished the lunchtime rush and left the shop in the capable hands of the apprentice, Katy.

Waving at Mark and Peter, Lizzy couldn't help but grin. She hadn't been ice skating since she was a teenager, but she was really looking forward to hitting the ice just like they used to when they were younger.

"Hey guys!" Claire said as she caught up to them. "Are you ready for some fun on the ice?"

"I'll probably put the skates on and completely forget how to balance, then fall flat on my face!" said

Peter, grimacing, while Mark looked similarly bashful and nodded in agreement.

"Don't be silly! You're a natural on the ice — both of you are!" Lizzy admonished Peter and Mark.

"Come on," said Claire. "Let's get inside out of this snow."

They lined up and paid the entry fee. While they stood in the queue, a sign on the wall sparked Lizzy's attention.

"Locker room — that's it!"

Claire turned to Lizzy in puzzlement. "What about the locker room?"

"It's where my next Santa clue will be hidden. I'm going to go and have a look before going on the ice. I won't be long; you guys go ahead and I'll join you in a moment."

"Oh, I'll give you a hand if you like?" Peter said as Claire and Mark made their way to the skate hire counter.

The locker room had had a re-paint since the last time Lizzy had been there. In fact, from what she could see through the glass doors to the ice, the whole facility had been refurbished.

Lizzy and Peter searched high and low in each locker and under the benches but couldn't find a clue.

"Perhaps Santa is running a little late with his mail today," Peter joked.

With a disappointed look on her face, Lizzy shrugged and walked out into the foyer to hire a pair of skates. Once they had switched their boots for skates, Lizzy and Peter walked onto the skating rink to find Claire and Mark. They were by a fire pit in the centre of the rink, huddled together drinking hot chocolate and reminiscing about their school days.

"Do you remember that time when we attempted to get Liam and Steph together for graduation?" Claire was saying. "I can't remember why our plan backfired, but I know Steph was not happy with us. Do you know, it took her two months until she would talk to me again!"

"Oh yes, that plan didn't work because none of us realised that Liam is hopeless on the ice. He spent the whole time sitting in the café, so none of us had seen him attempt to skate." Mark roared with laughter.

They continued their reminiscing while Peter and Lizzy gingerly completed a few laps of the rink. Seeing a friend on the other side of the rink, Peter excused himself and skated over to have a chat. Lizzy was contemplating returning to the locker room to have another look for the letter when she saw Mark and Claire looking very cosy, heads close, holding hands, gazing into each other's eyes as they skated around, completely oblivious to everyone around them.

So much for my childhood crush being my Secret Santa! Lizzy mused. *He seems very content with my best friend. Huh, some best friend she is – she knows I like Mark!*

Lizzy hadn't realised, but tears were tracking their way down her rosy cheeks. Needing some fresh air, she hastily made her way over to the benches, pulled her skates off, put her boots back on and ran out of the rink into the cold winter air.

Before she knew what was happening, Lizzy had crashed into a solid object and was on the floor, but something or someone had cushioned her fall. Shaking her head to clear her tear-blurred vision, Lizzy's eyes met eyes the deepest shade of blue she had ever seen. They resembled the ocean on a summer's day; they were mesmerising. All of a sudden, the owner of the ocean-blue eyes spoke.

"Liz, are you okay? What's wrong? Why are you crying?" Peter gazed up from underneath her with concern etched all over his face.

Jumping up, Lizzy wiped her tears on her sleeves and, avoiding eye contact with Peter, turned to run off. Peter, however, had guessed what she was about to do and grabbed the sleeve of her coat.

"Liz, look at me," he pleaded, turning Lizzy's chin up so her eyes met his again.

"Please, Peter, I can't go into it now, I just want to go home," Lizzy begged, fresh tears streaming down her cheeks.

Peter looked deep into her eyes and slowly raised a hand to brush the tears from her cheeks with the pad of his thumb.

"Come on, I'll take you home." Peter put his arm around her shoulders, guided Lizzy to her car and drove the two miles in silence back to her house.

Upon opening the front door, Lizzy flung her coat over the banister, flopped down on the sofa in front of the fire and sobbed uncontrollably, leaving Peter standing in the doorway unsure of what to do.

"How could she, Peter?" Lizzy growled. "How can she blatantly flirt with Mark in front of me when she knows I've always liked him?"

"Wait, what? You like my brother?" Peter gasped, wide eyed.

Ignoring Peter's comment, Lizzy continued sobbing. Peter sat down next to her and engulfed her in his strong arms, carefully stroking her hair whilst whispering gentle reassurances in her ear.

"Speak to Claire in the morning. She probably didn't realise what she was doing or how much you like Mark."

"I don't know how I feel about anything any-more — I'm so confused!" Lizzy wailed as her tears continued to fall, soaking the shoulder of Peter's shirt.

Kissing the top of her head, Peter sat still and continued to reassure her until she drifted off to sleep in his arms.

***

A few hours later, Lizzy stirred, feeling secure and safe. Slowly, she opened her eyes to find herself in the arms of a sleeping Peter. Craning her neck to look over the back of the couch out of the window, she saw it was already dark outside. That's when the memories of what had occurred at the ice rink came flooding back. Reality dawned on her: Mark couldn't be Santa; he was too engrossed with Claire to even know Lizzy was at the rink. In hindsight, it had been obvious for quite some time really. The two of them would always migrate to each other at events, and whenever they went out as a group of friends, Mark always insisted on taking Claire home. How had Lizzy missed the signs? How had she not recognised the look they exchanged whenever they caught sight of each other? It was a look of adoration and longing. Had she been so blinded by her own feelings for Mark that she hadn't realised what was going on right under her nose?

The part that shocked Lizzy the most was that Claire hadn't confided in her at all. Why? Was it because she knew Lizzy had a crush on Mark and didn't want to wreck her dreams? Or was it because of the Secret Santa vow of silence she had agreed to? As Mark was on the list, if Claire had announced her relationship with Mark, that would have narrowed the list of Santa suspects down too quickly. However, that must mean that Mark was in on the Santa secret to not reveal anything about their relationship either.

Lizzy mentally reviewed the situation; she was left with just one possibility. Frozen in realisation, Lizzy didn't know what to do.

Peter was Santa! All the clues slotted into place like a jigsaw puzzle.

Desperately needing to escape the situation she was in, Lizzy gently manoeuvred Peter's arm from her shoulder, placing it in his lap as she rose from the sofa, and tiptoed out the room. Grabbing her handbag and car keys, she left a brief note stating that she needed some time to think but would be back when she was ready to face Claire and Mark. She crept out of the house, hurriedly scraped the ice and snow from her car windscreen and side windows and jumped into the driver's seat.

She didn't know where she was heading, but anywhere was better than the village and the sight of Mark, Claire and Peter. It wasn't until the headlights of an oncoming car blinded her that she realised she had been driving on autopilot for the last fifteen minutes. Upon looking around at the countryside, now covered in a blanket of white, Lizzy slowly recognised where she was. She was heading north along the winding mountain road that led to the little town of Hammerton. The road, running parallel to a stream, meandered through the mountain valley. It was a wonderful landscape where she would often go hiking along the trails in the summer months.

At the top of a hill, Lizzy spotted a service station. She pulled in and filled up the fuel tank and picked up some food and drinks for the journey. She had no idea where she was heading or how long she would be gone, but she needed to clear her head and make a decision on how she was going to move forward with her life.

Further along the road, Lizzy pulled into a deserted car park overlooking the stream. The picturesque scene looked like a Christmas card as the snow continued to fall around her.

Lizzy knew that she had no real reason to be mad at Mark and Claire; they had obviously been sworn to secrecy by Peter so he could fully implement his plan. It was herself she was angry with, and she knew the reason why, she was just too scared to admit it.

She never felt safer and more loved than she did in Peter's arms.

Lizzy recalled occasions she had passed off as a love/hate, brother/sister relationship, when he would tease her, put frogs in her schoolbag, beat her in snowball fights and argue the toss over her choice of boyfriends, but upon looking back, she realised that it was actually love. She was in love with Peter Henley, and he was in love with her!

How had she not realised this sooner? Not wanting to waste any more time, Lizzy turned over the engine. She felt compelled to get to Peter as quickly as she could. Unfortunately, her car — or more so the snow — had other ideas. While she had been gazing at the view trying to make sense of her life, Lizzy hadn't noticed the snow begin to fall more heavily, to the extent that it now swirled around in gusts, creating snowdrifts. The car was half-buried; she couldn't get it to move and she couldn't open any of the doors to get out.

Panicking, her body went into autopilot. She located her mobile phone and dialled the number of the first name she thought of… Peter!

The dial tone had barely rung once when it was answered by a very flustered Peter.

"Liz? Where are you? Are you okay? I've been worried sick, you just disappeared and the snow has started coming down thick and fast. I thought something had happened to you!"

Lizzy could hear the panic and anxiety in his voice.

"I haven't got time to explain, but I'm stuck in a snowdrift and I can't open the car doors." Tears began to spill over her cheeks, and her voice trembled as her teeth chattered together in her body's natural effort to get warm.

"Okay, Liz, I'm coming to find you. Where are you?"

"I'm stuck on the road between the village and Hammerton, in a car park overlooking the stream. Please help me, Peter — it's freezing in here, and I hate to admit it but I'm really scared!"

Taking on his more calm, cool and collected manner, Peter gave Lizzy instructions on how to keep as warm as she could and promised to come and find her quickly.

Hanging up the phone, Peter grabbed some food, blankets, a shovel and a thermos of hot chocolate, threw everything into the truck and dashed out of the village as fast as he safely could in the snowy weather. Luckily, he had chained his wheels the day before when the first cold spell began, meaning he could make good ground along the icy roads.

Desperate to know she was okay, Peter called Lizzy and left his phone on speaker on the passenger seat. The ring tone went on for what seemed like ages, but he heard a click as Lizzy answered the call.

"Lizzy, can you hear me?" he shouted, deep concern etched in his voice as the signal started cutting out.

"Yes, I can just about hear you, Peter, but I don't think I will for long. I can't see anything out of the windows anymore — I think I am completely buried in the snow!"

Peter's anxiety reached an all-time high. If the car was completely buried, it wouldn't be long before the oxygen in it was used up, leaving Lizzy to suffocate. He couldn't lose her, not now he was so close to telling her the truth: how much he had loved her since they were children, and how he wanted to be with her for the rest of his life because she made him whole. He was only truly happy when Lizzy was with him. It had taken a lot of convincing on Mark and Claire's part, but they had persuaded him to finally admit his feelings and declare his love. The Secret Santa idea had come about from his nervousness of telling Lizzy to her face. He didn't want to risk seeing her look of horror as he told her the truth. It would break his heart, and he didn't think he could get over it if she rejected him.

"I'm nearly with you, Liz. Hold on, keep talking to me!" Peter shouted at the phone.

Knowing that she was really in trouble, Lizzy decided to apologise to him. "Peter, I lied to you, I'm sorry." Taking a deep breath and closing her eyes, Lizzy continued. She realised the air was getting thin inside her snow prison, which meant she might not hold out until Peter reached her. "I didn't know what I wanted, but I realised that Santa wasn't who I first wished it to be."

Feeling herself gasping for breath and struggling to keep her eyes open and focused, she could hear Peter whispering, pleading with God to spare her.

"Peter, I feel really sleepy, I'm just going to close my eyes for a short time until you reach me. I'm sorry."

With that, the phone connection died, leaving Peter distraught behind the wheel, tears streaming down his cheeks.

"No! Lizzy, wake up! You have to stay awake. Stay with me, Lizzy. Lizzy, can you hear me? Lizzy? I love you!"

Peter floored the accelerator. He had to reach Lizzy before it was too late. He had to save her; he'd dreamed all his life of marrying her, having children and living happily ever after. Everything he'd ever dreamed of now rested in his hands.

CHAPTER THIRTEEN

Finally, Peter pulled into the car park. He could just make out the roof of Lizzy's car protruding from the top of the snowdrift. Grabbing the shovel, Peter launched himself out of the truck and frantically began digging the car out of the snow, all the while shouting above the swirling gusts of wind and snow.

"Liz, I'm here. Don't die on me now, love, please wake up. Please, I couldn't bear it if you left me! Oh, Lizzy, please, please, please be okay!"

After a few minutes that felt like a lifetime, Peter had managed to clear the snow around one of the back doors. He prised the door open, which was not an easy task as the ice and snow had frozen it shut, and climbed in the back of the car.

The sight he was met with sent a chill down his spine. Lizzy was slumped over the steering wheel, unconscious. Peter knew he had to get her out and into the warmth of his truck, quickly.

Desperately, Peter shook her shoulder, calling for her to wake up. After receiving no response, he realised he would have to pull her from the car and carry her to the truck.

Gently lifting Lizzy under her arms and legs, Peter pulled her over the driver's seat and into his lap. He checked she was still breathing, then tore his jacket off and wrapped it around her the best he could.

Taking her in his arms, Peter stumbled through the snow-laden car park to his truck. He lay her down in the passenger seat and trudged round the front of the truck to jump into the driver's seat. Peter grabbed the blanket from the back seat and wrapped it around Lizzy. The movement made her stir, and she blinked to regain her focus so she could make out her rescuer.

"Pete?" she murmured.

"Hush, Liz, don't talk. Yes, it's me, I've got you now — you're safe!" Peter comforted her as he turned the engine over to kickstart the heating system. Watching a small smile appear on Lizzy's lips, he knew she would be fine.

Strapping them both in, Peter put the truck in gear and pulled out of the car park onto the snow-covered road.

Carefully, he manoeuvred the truck around snow-drifts and tree branches that had broken and fallen under the weight of the snow. The snow continued to fall heavily, making it difficult to see more than a few feet in front of the truck.

"Are we nearly home yet?" Lizzy mumbled, her eyes still closed in her blanket cocoon.

"Unfortunately, the roads are thick with snow, so I'm having to take it very slowly. We should be home in two to three hours," Peter explained, glancing over at Lizzy.

Accepting the explanation and murmuring an inaudible response, Lizzy shifted her positioning under the blanket and drifted off to sleep.

Ninety minutes later, she suddenly opened her eyes in confusion, panic written on her face, and sat bolt upright. The blanket fell into her lap.

"What happened? Where am I?"

Startled by her sudden actions, Peter tried to reassure her. "Don't worry, Liz. We have about an hour or so left until we reach home. You're safe with me." He offered her a comforting smile.

"Oh, Peter, thank you for rescuing me. I didn't know the snow had got so thick so fast. I was so scared; I didn't think you would make it in time," Lizzy rambled, desperate to get her words out and explain what she was thinking when she ran away, leaving him asleep on her sofa.

"Lizzy, I would move heaven and Earth to get to you. I don't know what I'd do without you in my life," Peter admitted, glancing briefly at Lizzy before turning his head back towards the road. "Let's get you home so you can warm up by the fire."

The remainder of the journey took an hour. The snow was still coming down thickly and settling in small drifts all along the road.

Pulling into Lizzy's driveway, Peter turned off the engine and walked around the truck to help Lizzy out.

He opened the front door, guided Lizzy inside and settled her on the sofa. The fire had long since burned out, so there was a chill in the air. Ensuring Lizzy was comfortable and still covered with the blanket, Peter tended to the fireplace and within minutes had a roaring fire burning in the hearth. He headed to the kitchen and busied himself preparing food and drinks for the both of them. Lizzy watched him silently as he returned with a tray of hot chocolate and Christmas cookies. Handing a mug to Lizzy, Peter settled on the sofa beside her.

Lizzy took a long sip from her mug and hugged it to her in an attempt to warm her hands. Unsure how to broach the subject, she stayed quiet while she tried to gather her thoughts and work out how to explain herself.

The silence was obviously too much for him, and after a few minutes of awkwardness, he asked the inevitable question she'd hoped to avoid.

"So, what was going through your mind, to just get up and run off like that? I was worried sick!"

Lizzy had the foresight to keep her eyes front, staring into the dancing flames in the fireplace. Her feelings were quite raw at the moment, and she hadn't quite got her head around the recent revelations.

"I'm sorry, Peter, I really don't know. I panicked, I suppose. Mark and Claire upset me and sent me into a complete spiral of confusion as I had thought Mark was Santa. I just needed to clear my head and try to make sense of everything." Lizzy chanced a glance in Peter's direction to find he was also staring into the fire.

Content with the feeling of safety emanating from him, Lizzy snuggled down into the sofa and leant her head on the armrest, watching the flames dance and lick the charred logs. The warmth of the fire and flickering light steadily lulled her into a dreamless sleep. The next thing she knew, Peter was shaking her shoulder to wake her.

"Liz, come on, you better head on up to bed. You fell asleep. I'll call you tomorrow and check you're okay. Night, night." Peter smiled, leaning over and planting a small kiss on her forehead before rising from the sofa, donning his coat and heading out into the cold night.

Drowsy, Lizzy turned off the light, locked the door after Peter and went upstairs to bed.

CHAPTER FOURTEEN

Slowly opening her eyes against the bright light streaming in from the partially opened curtains, Lizzy rolled over onto her back and stared at the ceiling.

Thoughts flashed through her head of the previous day, how near she'd come to disaster and how being in that situation had forced her mind to come to a startling realisation. She was in love with Peter, her best friend since childhood, the guy who'd always had her back but at the same time given her grief, as brothers and sisters do. Looking back through their friendship, Lizzy realised how many situations clearly proved that Peter was hiding his feelings for her: the way he looked at her, how he reacted around her boyfriends, how he had never really had any girlfriends. How could she have been so blind? They had been best friends for so long, their friendship was almost habitual, to the point that Lizzy knew she could not live a single day without him.

Realising what day it was, Lizzy jumped out of bed and ran downstairs to the kitchen, where the advent calendar stood on the counter. Remembering the note from the other day, Lizzy opened the last door, her hand trembling with anticipation. What she pulled out sent tears rolling down her cheeks in shock.

Opening up the black velvet box, Lizzy gasped as her eyes met a glistening diamond ring on a blue cushion. Placing the box on the kitchen counter, Lizzy unfolded the note.

My dearest Lizzy,

The day has come, Christmas Eve. By now, you have probably guessed my identity, but just in case you're not sure, what I am about to write will leave you under no illusions.

As you know, I am deeply in love with you and I have been since we were children. You are my whole world, Lizzy, and I don't think I would be able to cope if you weren't a part of it.

Seeing other guys break your heart so many times broke my heart too, to see how upset you were. I could never understand how they could treat such an amazing, caring, lovable person like you the way they did. All I wanted to do was wrap you up in my arms and protect you from the world.

I have sat on the sidelines all my life, observing you, supporting you and giving you advice when you have asked for it. I live for the moments we share together, either alone or with our other friends.

It has taken me this long to admit my feelings, which is why I have decided to do this in a letter when I'm not present for two reasons:

1. *So you can absorb the information at your own pace and you can think about it for as long as you need to without me staring at you, hoping you will say yes.*

2. *You do not have to say no to my face, because I know I won't be able to take it.*

Therefore, please answer me in one of the following ways:

If you agree, put on the ring and come and make your Christmas wish to Santa at the children's hospital.

If you do not agree, please keep the ring, but I will know you do not want to progress with this relationship because you will not turn up to see Santa. I promise to never mention it again, and I hope we can remain friends.

So here it is, the question that has been on the tip of my tongue for years.

Elizabeth Chesterfield, will you make me the happiest man alive and agree to become Mrs Claus? Will you marry me?

I hope against all hope that I see you today!

All my love,

Santa (Peter) xx

Lizzy re-read the letter what felt like one hundred times. Tears of joy continued to cascade down her cheeks. Slowly, she removed the ring from the blue cushion and considered her decision. She loved Peter. Deep down, she had always had feelings for him; she just hadn't fully understood them. Staring at the ring as it sparkled in the light of the kitchen, Lizzy knew what she wanted to do. It was a no-brainer. Slowly, she pushed the ring onto her finger. It fit like a glove, and she wondered how Peter had known her ring size, but she could find those trivial details out later on. For now, she had a proposal to accept. Glancing up at the clock on the kitchen wall, Lizzy was surprised to see it was already 10:30 a.m.

She almost tripped on the top stair in her excitement as she ran two at a time back up to the bathroom to shower and get ready.

After a considerable amount of time spent rummaging through her drawers and wardrobe to find something suitable to wear, Lizzy realised she didn't need to dress up in anything special for Peter. He had seen her in her Sunday best, in her pyjamas, in fancy dress costumes and pretty much every item of clothing she possessed. Settling for practical jeans, a dress shirt, jumper and boots, Lizzy ran back downstairs, grabbed her keys and ran out of the house, struggling to get her coat, hat, scarf and gloves on as she rushed down the path towards the bus stop.

***

As much as Peter enjoyed seeing the awestruck faces of the children as he went from ward to ward handing out presents and spending a few minutes with each child hearing their Christmas wishes, the Santa suit was starting to make him itch. Glancing up at a clock on the wall above a nurse's station, he sighed as he tried to come to terms with the fact that Lizzy was turning him down. She hadn't appeared to accept his proposal, and it was now 11:45 a.m. He only had another fifteen minutes to head down to the foyer and pose for photos with some children who had won a Christmas colouring competition.

The foyer was decorated in red and gold with a large, eight-foot tree in the centre. It was under the tree that a throne had been set up for him to sit upon with the children sitting on his knee for the picture. He greeted the children who were all waiting patiently in line and repeated the same questions he had been asking all morning: "What would you like for Christmas? Have you been a good boy or girl? How are you spending Christmas day?" Repeating the same lines on autopilot eventually made Peter space out slightly. He smiled for the camera when it was required and made the right noises in response to the children's wishes, but by the time the last child was approaching, he wasn't even paying attention to the faces around him. He just wanted to get out of the suit, drive back home, close the door and shut himself off from the world so he could wallow in his own self-pity, as he had most definitely ruined the best relationship he had ever had. His friendship with Lizzy. There was no way she would want to be around him after this whole debacle.

What brought him slightly out of his reverie was the weight of the last child as they perched on his knee and placed their arms around his neck. It was only as she spoke in answer to his question "What would you like for Christmas?" that he turned his full attention to her.

"I only have one wish for Christmas, and that is to set a date for my wedding, because the best man in the world proposed to me this morning by letter and I want to say yes and have him place the ring on my finger. I want to finally kiss him and tell him how much I love him, that I hadn't realised it, but I think I have always loved him, and finally I want to plan our life together." Lizzy smiled, tears of happiness glistening in the corners of her eyes, threatening to spill over as she waited for Peter's reply.

As he stared at her in complete shock, it took a few moments for Lizzy's words to fully sink in. Lizzy could see the exact moment on his features when realisation dawned. Unable to string a coherent sentence together, Peter stared, open mouthed as she beamed at him. Peter's eyes met hers with one raised, questioning eyebrow.

Lizzy glanced round the room to make sure no children were still around, then, seeing the coast was clear, she tugged down Peter's fake beard, nodded and smiled in response to his unspoken question and pressed her lips softly to his.

Finally, Peter was shocked out of his trance and took the opportunity to envelop Lizzy in a hug as they both poured all the love, admiration, want and need that they both had for one another into the kiss. Neither was left with any doubt once they pulled apart, but Peter just had to clear one niggling question that had come to the forefront of his mind.

"Can I ask you a question?" he gingerly enquired, not able to make eye contact.

"Of course!"

"You implied last night that you had feelings for my brother. Are you quite sure you love me, and it wasn't just the relief of feeling safe with me that made you say it?" Peter winced, hoping against all hope that the answer was what he wanted to hear.

Grabbing Peter by the shoulders, Lizzy pulled him round to face her. She peered into his deep blue eyes.

"I'll admit that at school I had a crush on Mark, but so did every girl in our year! It was seeing Claire with Mark yesterday that made me realise that you were Santa. I'll also admit that it freaked me out at first, so much so that I had to get out of the village, away from you and everyone else to clear my head." Lifting her hands up to cup his cheeks, Lizzy made sure what she was about to say would be completely understood without a shadow of a doubt. "While stranded in the car surrounded by snow, the only person I thought of was you. You are my world, and I can't live without you. I didn't realise what I was feeling until I thought it was too late. I love you, Peter Henley, and I always will. If you'll have me, I want to spend the rest of my life with you!"

Beaming, Peter placed a hand on each of Lizzy's cheeks and planted a soft, gentle kiss on her lips.

"I can't think of anything I would prefer than to get married, raise a family and grow old with you. Let me go and change out of this costume, then do you want to go and grab a hot chocolate at the coffee shop?"

Nodding in agreement, Lizzy stood to allow Peter to rise out of the chair and head towards the changing room. She waited for five minutes until Peter emerged in his usual jeans, T-shirt and dress shirt. The blue and white checked pattern brought out the deep blue of his eyes.

Peter grabbed Lizzy's hand as they walked out of the foyer and into the cold street. The snow, although it was still falling steadily and was settling on all surfaces, had calmed down massively. Neither of them could keep the full-blown grins from brightening up their faces. As they arrived at the coffee shop, Peter opened the door and held it open for Lizzy. At the ringing of the bell above the door, Claire looked up from the cake she was slicing up on the counter and smiled at the sight that greeted her: Peter and Lizzy walking into the shop, hand in hand, with smiles bursting from ear to ear.

"So, Santa, I take it she said yes?" Claire nodded towards Lizzy's left hand.

"Yes, she did!" Peter smiled, meeting Lizzy's gaze. "Claire, thank you for keeping my secret. I know it was a lot to ask as you and Lizzy share everything."

"Peter, me and Mark have sat and watched you both dance around each other, pretending you don't have feelings for each other for years, even if you didn't realise what those feelings were." Claire smiled at Lizzy, who was a little surprised by her friend's admission.

"Why didn't you tell me you and Mark were an item?" Lizzy admonished Claire.

"If I'd told you, it would have given the Santa secret away. In fact, Santa was mine and Mark's idea. It was obvious that Peter was never going to admit his feelings to you without a push in the right direction." Claire smirked as Mark entered the coffee shop.

"Hey, what have I missed?" he asked as he went over to Claire, gave her a peck on the cheek and slipped his arm around her waist.

"These two have finally admitted their feelings to each other, and you are about to gain a sister-in-law," Claire explained.

"Hey, that's great! Congratulations!" Swinging his arm around Peter's shoulders and pulling him into a side hug, Mark smiled at his little brother. "See, what did Claire and I tell you? We could see she was smitten with you, and you didn't believe us!"

Rolling his eyes and looking sheepishly towards the floor, Peter mumbled, "I wanted to believe you. I hoped beyond all hope that what you said was true, but I didn't want to risk losing Lizzy for good by opening my mouth and making things awkward between us."

Lizzy gently lifted his chin up with a finger so her eyes met his, boring down deep into his soul so there was no doubt in Peter's mind.

"You would never lose me, Peter Henley. Don't ever be afraid to talk to me. You're stuck with me for life now!"

Slowly, the grin reappeared on Peter's face as he wound his arms around Lizzy's waist, pulling her into a bone-crushing hug, planting sweet kisses on her lips.

In between kisses, Peter told her, "I don't think you realise how happy you've made me; my dreams are coming true. I love you so much!"

It was in that moment that they both knew they had found their soulmate and would lead long and happy lives together.

THE END

PUBLISHER INFORMATION

Rowanvale Books provides publishing services to independent authors, writers and poets all over the globe. We deliver a personal, honest and efficient service that allows authors to see their work published, while remaining in control of the process and retaining their creativity. By making publishing services available to authors in a cost-effective and ethical way, we at Rowanvale Books hope to ensure that the local, national and international community benefits from a steady stream of good quality literature.

For more information about us, our authors or our publications, please get in touch.

www.rowanvalebooks.com
info@rowanvalebooks.com

Printed in Great Britain
by Amazon